The Arrogant Death of Dr. Jones

by
Stephen Hufman M.D.

-

ISBN 978-1-7336456-2-1

To Matt Bangsund and the Amigos who
taught me so much about living.

Table of Contents

Chapter 1 - Death the Beginning

This story starts at the gravestone of Dr. Thomas Jones Jr., for often it is the ending that becomes the beginning. Etched in stone is a poem and three Bible verses about learning to breathe. Something for all his education Dr. Jones had neglected to learn.

"I thought I knew the way,
then death came and took my breath away.
My pride would not suffice,
where His glory paid the price."

Dr. Thomas Jones Jr. 1949 - 2012

"What good is it for a man to gain the whole world, yet forfeit his soul?" Matthew 16:26

"Lowborn men are but a breath, the high-born are but a lie; if weighed on a balance, they are nothing; together they are only a breath." Psalm 62:9

"Now these three remain: Faith, Hope, and Love." 1 Corinthians 13:13

My Turn

In 2005 Thomas Jones had reached the pinnacle of success. By every standard he had achieved the highest levels of medicine. Now, flying back to his alma mater to have a building named for him, he could hardly contain himself. Looking out through the airplane's window at the sprawling land below he whispered, "I have it all." Breathing deeply of this moment, he gazed again at the gold embossed invitation from the university.

May 22, 2005 at 2:00 PM, University Medical Plaza

University Medical School Graduation

Commencement speaker: the esteemed Dr. Thomas Jones Jr.

Founder of the TJ Genetics Institute

Followed by the dedication of the Thomas Jones Center for Genetics Research

Thomas slipped the announcement back into the leather folder that held his speech. It irked him that they had dropped the Jr. from the center's name. He understood the reason in an aesthetic sense, but it made him question if he would ever be free of his father's shadow. As a medical student, he often walked by the portrait of his father hanging in the library and felt the stern presence of the man. This memory triggered a cascade of upsetting thoughts... *Why am I so affected by a person who has been dead for over thirty years? He was never there for me, so why do I let him trouble me now?* This set off a litany of self-reproach... *You'll never measure up to your dad... You could do more if you just applied yourself. Why can't you be like your father? He gave medicine everything... You'll always be second rate...*

NO! Thomas yelled at the voices in his head. *I've put in the hard work and the sacrifice that medicine demands... This is silly. I will not let the memory of my dad spoil this day!* Thomas shook himself from these distressing thoughts, straightened his tie, and took a deep breath trying to relax. *This is my turn, and no one will take it from me.* He then shifted in his seat and looked out the window, forcing his attention onto the good things about to take place. His mind latched onto a wonderful thought—he had invited his estranged daughter, Robin, to attend as his honored guest. They had not seen each other in years, though that was not his fault. His ex-wife had prevented Robin from coming to see him after he had moved to Washington, though he had not fought this too hard since his research consumed most of his days. Even phone calls became infrequent because of their busy schedules. But now he would see her again and make up for lost time. Thomas hoped that when Robin saw all the tributes and amazing medical breakthroughs his efforts had accomplished, she would understand his absences and be proud of him.

The plane began to bounce and the seat belt sign blinked on. Thomas glanced out the window to see what had caused the turbulence, but all he could see was a drab disorienting grayness. *Relax,* he told himself, *we're just going through a cloud.*

Thomas checked his watch. *We should land within the hour.* His excitement continued to build. He exhaled. *Slow down… breathe easy…*

nothing is going to take this moment from you. This will be your glorious return in triumph. Settling back into the seat, he pulled out his speech to review the words he would say at the commencement. This set Thomas to daydreaming of his years in medical school, of all the long hours of study and striving, just to be worthy of being called a doctor. *But I exceeded all expectations,* he reminded himself. Suddenly a thought popped up. *Even my father would be forced to say, "Well done."*

Thomas grew up the only child of Dr. Thomas Jones Sr., a pediatric neurosurgeon, famous for separating twins conjoined at the head and for pioneering many other surgeries. He had set the bar high and pushed Thomas hard to achieve great things.

"You can do better than that," his father would often say, followed by, "Remember our family doesn't settle for being good, when with a little more effort you will be the best."

Thomas could hear that raspy voice criticizing all that did not measure up to his father's standard of perfection. During Thomas' first year of medical school, an auto-accident cut short his dad's life, ending what little relationship they had. This made the burden of being the son of the great Dr. Thomas Jones even more oppressive. The shadow of his dad's legacy never left and pushed Thomas to keep going when others quit. Yet, it also made it hard to breathe because things were never quite good enough. *But not today! This is my day to shine.*

"We should be on the ground in thirty minutes," the intercom interrupted his thoughts. "Attendants, please begin cabin pickup in preparation for landing."

Thomas handed the half-eaten breakfast tray to the first-class cabin attendant. "Was there anything wrong with your breakfast, Dr. Jones?" she asked taking the food tray.

"No, no, I… a… I've been looking forward to this day for quite a while and I'm eager to get going." He covered his mouth, trying to stifle a "buurrp." He loosened his tie and shifted over to the window, gazing at the passing scenery. The gray clouds had cleared and snow-covered peaks dazzled in the morning sun. The mountains stood at attention to honor his return. His mind sifted through the memories of those years of relentless study and sacrifice, of constantly pushing himself to be the top of his class in medical school. He had watched the sun rise above the mountains many times from the medical school library, thinking, *Someday I'll return, and you'll be looking up at me.* Thomas mentally reviewed all he had accomplished in his career. Who knew how many lives he had helped with his groundbreaking gene research? He visualized the long list of awards and accomplishments that would be on the plaque next to his portrait in the library. *Yes, everyone, would have to agree I've done well...*

A voice came over the intercom. "We will make our final pick-up before landing. Please return your seats and tray tables to their upright position and put away anything you may have taken out for the flight."

As the plane swooped down upon the city, Thomas searched the houses below for clues to locate the place where he had grown up. So much had changed in the last forty years. There, among the crisscrossing streets, he saw the elementary school and two blocks south stood his old house. *Yes, that's where it all started.* His thoughts sparkled with the morning sun. Slipping his hand

12

into his front pocket, he fiddled with something wrapped in a worn handkerchief and gave it a gentle squeeze. The cloth held a special symbol of the driving force behind all the effort and sacrifice that preceded this auspicious occasion. Sitting back he breathed, "I have finally reached the capstone of my life."

The Gift

Closing his eyes, Thomas could see his old schoolyard and nearby playing field surrounded by a chain-link fence. Every day after school, he had to run the gauntlet of the bully Carl Knox and his gang. Thomas knew to avoid eye contact and just get through, ignoring their taunts. Sometimes, Thomas would hang back waiting for another kid to be the object of their bullying so he could slip by unnoticed. Even in this daydream, the thought of Carl's voice made him sweat.

"Teeny-weeny Tommy-go-run-to-Mommy," Carl teased. The others would laugh and join in.

"Little Tom Thumb lookout you bum," accompanied by a kick to his bottom.

"Tommy tears, you're a crybaby… what's-a-matter; need your diaper changed?"

Thomas hated the teasing because no matter how hard he fought it, the taunting always made him cry.

As a child, Thomas never measured up to the other boys in his class. Small for his age and uncoordinated, no one ever wanted him on their team. How many times he had watched from the sidelines and dreamed of hitting a home run to win the game, or being able to run fast, beyond anyone's reach, and score a touchdown. *One of these days I'll be the one everyone wants to be around. They'll wish for what I have and wonder how the one they laughed at could have achieved so much.*

Thomas continued looking from the plane window for one specific street corner near the school. *Yes, there it is.* His mind whirled with the memory of what took place there while walking home. He could still hear the ugly voices of those boys yelling names.

"Hey dummy!"

"Stupid!"

"Pea-brain!"

On one pivotal day, Thomas remembered flinching at hearing the taunts from Carl and his friends, knowing that even worse teasing would follow. He kept his head down and ran to an oak tree to hide. Grabbing some acorns to throw, he slumped behind the tree. Peeping out from the trunk, he expected to see his tormentors moving toward him. But on this day, they were picking on someone else. Thomas at first froze. *They don't know I'm here!* Calming himself with that thought, he sought to slink away unnoticed. Keeping a wary eye on the boys, he began his escape. They had formed a circle around the unfortunate recipient of their ridicule—a short squat boy from the Special Ed class. He wore thick glasses covering small eyes with a perpetual squint, pudgy cheeks and a protruding tongue between dried chapped lips. Thomas knew the boy's slowness made him an easy target for Carl and the others.

"Mybaackpaack," the kid cried, as he struggled to grab his pack, but the boys were throwing it to each other playing keep-away.

"Retard, retard, look at the little retard," they laughed and yelled, tossing the pack around.

Carl swung the pack and hit the kid in the face, knocking him to the sidewalk. Blood trickled from his nose.

"Hey Carl, you made the moron bleed… we'd better get out of here," said one of the gang.

Carl looked at his victim sitting on the ground trying to stop the bleeding with his hand. "Hey, Dunderhead, your mom made some mistake letting you be born." The boy lunged for his pack, but Carl yanked it away and drop-kicked it high in the air. It flopped to the ground at the feet of Thomas.

Carl started to run off with his friends when he noticed Thomas and stopped. With a menacing smirk he yelled, "You little twerp better not squeal, or I'll give you a bloody nose too." Thomas felt so scared that tears ran down his cheeks and his lower lip quivered. Carl took a step toward Thomas, then changed his mind. "What a wuss," He sneered. "Here's a friend for you." Laughing, Carl ran off yelling, "Dorky and porky, pudding and pie. Hit 'em in the nose and make them cry."

When the boys had left, Thomas picked up the kid's pack and handed it to him. As he did, Thomas noticed him trying to lick the blood from his upper lip. Tears mixed with blood dripped from his chin. Wiping his nose with his forearm only smeared the mess across his face. "Are you okay?" Thomas asked, giving the boy his handkerchief.

The boy tried to say something to Thomas in between sniffing back tears and blood, "Deyyy… sniff… baaaa… sniff… boooys."

"Huh? I don't understand," said Thomas, trying to sniff back his own tears.

"Meeean boooyyss," the boy said, holding the handkerchief to his nose.

Thomas shrugged, not sure what the boy had said as he turned to go.

"Taayoo," said the boy.

Thomas turned back to look. "I told you I don't understand. You'd better get on home before Carl comes back."

The boy held out the handkerchief to give it back. "No you keep it," Thomas said not wanting to touch the bloody mess. "You'll need it for your walk home."

Then the boy reached in his pocket, put something in the handkerchief, and shoved it into Thomas's hand. "Nooo, preeesen fooo yooou... Gwaadbwessyooou." Turning, he limped away dragging his pack.

Thomas stood and stared, ashamed he had done nothing to halt the teasing. After a few minutes of wrestling with his thoughts, Thomas looked down at his crumpled, blood-stained handkerchief. Inside the soiled cloth he found a toy lamb carved from wood.

"Some gift. Maybe it's what I deserve for being such a coward."

Stuffing them both in his pocket, he looked again at the boy. Thomas kicked a rock in anger... anger at Carl... anger at his own cowardice... anger at life for making disabled kids. "Someday I'll show them!" He shouted into the air.

Thomas shook himself free of the memory. "Well, that day is today," he affirmed, clenching his fist.

"Please turn off and stow all electronic devices as we are beginning our approach..." The overhead announcement brought Thomas from his musings.

Unexpected Detour

A smile broke out on Thomas' face as he pulled the old stained handkerchief out of his pocket. Wrapped inside nestled a toy lamb carved from wood. He placed it tucked down in his lap so no one would notice, fearing people wouldn't understand why a doctor had such a trinket. The features were worn smooth from constant fingering, and the right front leg had broken off. His eyes stared at the lamb. *Yes, everyone will know how well I have done with life after today. I believe I've earned it.*

The seatbelt sign blinked on with a bing. "Please fasten your seat belts in preparation for landing," said the flight attendant. "Seats and tray tables should be in their upright and locked position. All carry-ons should be stowed overhead or put under the seat in front of you. Thank you for your cooperation. We should be on the ground in fifteen minutes."

Thomas folded the handkerchief over the lamb and shoved it back in his pocket. He planned to pull it out during his speech and tell the audience the story of what had been the driving force in his career…. in life. Regaling the audience on how through grit and determination he had silenced the taunts of Carl. Thomas had been looking forward to this recognition for a long time, and now it was about to begin. There was something gratifying about returning to the medical school where you labored in obscurity but now honored above those professors who had demanded so much. Yes, they would finally look with admiration and maybe a little envy at what you've accomplished. Plus, all the current students would look and wonder if they too could someday climb to such lofty heights.

As the plane began the final approach, Thomas looked out over the city and saw the University Hospital across the valley sitting majestically on a hill above the rest of the city. So many memories, some good and some bad, but today he would savor the good.

As they docked at the gate, the plane engines shut down, the seatbelt sign blinked off, and the door opened.

Now on with the show! Thomas cheered to himself.

"Thank you for flying with us and please check for any personal belongings you may have…."

As he got up to leave, a sudden wave of nausea rolled up from his stomach. "Burrup." *Must be the breakfast omelet,* Thomas thought unconsciously rubbing his abdomen. Weakness engulfed his legs, and a tightness in his chest made it hard to breathe. *Get a grip on yourself. You can't throw up here. HOLD ON! It'll pass soon.* Making a great effort to stay in control, cold beads of sweat popped up on his forehead. *If I could just get some fresh air, I'll be better,* he told himself.

With great focus, he made it to the terminal gate and loosened his collar. Instead of feeling better, Thomas struggled to get his breath and tore at his collar. With each inhalation, heaviness tightened around his chest, and his legs became weak, ready to buckle. "No, not now," he gasped, collapsing to the floor, fighting to remain conscious. Far away, Thomas heard someone shout, "Someone call an ambulance!"

I can't breathe, I can't breathe. Thomas's lungs fought against the vice closing around his chest, but it would not release. Slowly he slipped away.

He knew he was having a heart attack. Thomas fought it with all his might. Suddenly, a strange lightness spread over him, like popping out of water to get a breath of air. This was accompanied by an odd sensation of leaving behind his body and floating above it all. The initial panic and struggle receded and gave way to thoughts of those waiting for him at the medical school.

It struck Thomas as ironic that his return to the University Hospital would be in an ambulance as a patient, or even more ironic, as a dead patient going to the morgue. A postmortem teaching case for pathology students. He envisioned the students standing encircling the table ready to begin, but this time he was on the dissecting table, instead of standing beside it. *Wait! Why am I thinking these ridiculous thoughts? I can't be dying.* Thomas looked down at his lifeless body. *NO, this is all wrong! Certainly I deserve better— look at all I have done in medicine…there must be some mistake!*

Thomas attempted to yell, but it stuck in his throat. Shaking off the morbid vision of a morgue, Thomas berated himself for letting this magnificent day slip away—robbed by a defective heart. "Why now? Why this way? My God! Is there no justice?" His voice barely audible.

"Is that a prayer?" came a voice cutting through the commotion.

Quickly Thomas turned to see who spoke those words, ready to unleash a verbal lashing at such sarcasm. But what met his eyes eclipsed what he expected. It was not the steward or a paramedic, but grayness on the fringe of daylight with no sense of depth or direction. A vast space of nothing.

"What's going on?" Thomas exclaimed. Turning back to his original direction, he glimpsed a frantic scene of medics working over a prone body near gate C-11. People in the airport stopped to gape but then moved on to their own direction.

"Another amp of epi… charge to 360, all clear, shock… no pulse, resume CPR… Someone put in an ET tube, keep his airway open…" shouted the EMT.

When Thomas turned his head away, the sounds grew quiet, and the scene flipped to an expanse of endless gray. It was like changing channels on a TV. One channel was tuned to a medical drama, the other white noise.

Quickly he turned back to the familiar, hoping to return and get on with life. The scene was now of ongoing CPR in an ambulance, with lights flashing and sirens blaring, racing toward the University Hospital. "O-two sat 85% and dropping; still no pulse, rhythm v-tach, alert the ER of our ETA... another amp of epi... charging paddles."

This time Thomas experienced a growing detachment, like a spectator hovering above the action. Staring down, he observed his body turning ashen like so many other patients he had watched die during his medical career.

How strange, Thomas thought, to float above my dying body. *Is this what it is like to be dead?* He had no panic or any bodily discomfort. His interest in the scene below ebbed, being replaced by curiosity over the gray surroundings. The ground stretched out gray in every direction—the sky gray, even the light, if you could call it that, a drab gray. Unable to reference any horizon, Thomas tried to take a step, but became disoriented, lost his balance and fell.

Chapter 2 - The Longing

"Father Abraham, have pity on me and send Lazarus to dip the tip of his finger in water and cool my tongue, because I am in agony in this fire." Luke 16:24

Lost in the Fog

Thomas hit the ground, striking his right shoulder, causing his head to bounce off the ground. He expected pain but felt very little other than a woozy sensation, like one being spun on a merry-go-round. Looking about, he saw nothing but a gray fog that gave him a foreboding sense of being lost. The mist seemed to tease out fears in Thomas, childish thoughts of monsters under the bed, and others more subtle like facing his father's disappointment. *Get a grip,* Thomas scolded himself. *There's a logical explanation. You'll get through this.* One fear resisted any attempt at being blocked—being alone.

Could I have been knocked out? Thomas reasoned. *I just need to wake up... of course, this is just a dream.* Shaking his head to clear the fogginess did nothing, except stir up dizziness. So, he lay still waiting for something... anything to happen. He searched for the horizon, but the color and texture of the ground blended into the atmosphere of mist. The ethereal light cast no shadows, making everything blend together into a gray nothingness. If not for feeling the rough stones beneath him, he would be totally disoriented as to up and down. Searching, he could find no hint as to his whereabouts. The air hung as bland and gray as the surroundings—not hot or cold, not even humid like one might expect in fog. Instead, only a nondescript emptiness spread out in every direction. Listening, he heard nothing but deafening silence that shouted of the things missing—day, night, wind... and any hint of life. *So this is what nonexistence feels like?* Thomas struggled with the thoughts of nothingness. *Stay calm, don't lose control; the worst thing you can do is panic.* Thomas tried to control his growing angst. *Where am I?... How long have I been here?* His mind strove to make sense of time and space, but that too began to slip away, lost in the gray mist. *I must remember who I am... a doctor... a scientist... I am Dr. Thomas Jones, geneticist. That's real, not this. Get ahold of yourself!... You can figure a way out of this. Maybe I'm in a coma waiting to wake up.* Again the silence began to weigh heavily on Thomas. *Will I ever wake up? Am I alive?... Do I even exist?* Thomas fought the chilling specter of being alone, with no end and no sense of anything to orient or anchor his mind. He knew of medical experiments where people, deprived of any sensation or external input to the brain, would hallucinate and eventually go crazy. His thoughts started to drift into the grayness before him. "Hold on," said Thomas aloud, his voice breaking the buzz of silence. "Use your brain. You can think your way through this…" But his words only faded into the stillness that engulfed him.

The initial disorientation from the fall had now left, replaced by a hollow feeling. Thomas looked at his hands to determine what injury he may have incurred from hitting the ground. "What is happening to me?" he shouted, staring at his arms in shock, for they were vague outlines in the grayness—with form, but little substance. Glancing at his legs and body made him catch his breath. They were mere variations of gray. *Am I a ghost? This must be a dream!* Quickly Thomas pulled his mind back from this apparition. *You're a doctor, think… logic,… careful deduction will get you through this… it has worked in the past and will work for you now.*

Sitting up, Thomas called out, "Hello? Is anybody there?" The sound of his voice seemed swallowed in the stillness. Twisting about, he no longer could view or hear anything from the ambulance. All of what came before began to drift into a distant memory.

I am losing the last remnants of… he searched for an elusive thought… *life! How do I know what is real?* A chill went through him as he reviewed an array of memories that constituted his sixty years: growing up, his medical career, the achievements and awards—but they felt lifeless, like an ancient mythical story.

"Buurup."

"A noise! Yes, now at least something." Thomas turned. It came from somewhere off to his left.

"Buuurruup."

Thomas strained to see what emitted such a gross sound. Suddenly, a whiff of something foul stung his nose. *Yuck!* It reminded him of the dead rotting fish his dog liked to roll in when they walked along the river.

Unexpectedly, the smell also brought nauseating visions of shameful things: wars, famine, debauchery of every sort. The stink shrouded everything in ugliness and pulled Thomas into dark thoughts of death. *What kind of abomination could cause such a sickening odor?* "Get away," Thomas yelled. "I can't breathe in such foulness… get out of here."

Looking around for a way of escape produced nothing but angst, for every direction smelled and whatever lay out there seemed to be drawing closer.

"Who's there?" Thomas looked around in growing apprehension.

"Buuurup." The sound unleashed another wave of nauseating gas. Followed by a slurping sound of someone licking their lips. A movement off to the side caught Thomas' attention. Squinting, he thought he saw a shadow hovering… a dark smudge in the fog. Something dreadful hovered just beyond his sight, waiting… for him.

"What do you want with me? You aren't real, you're just a bad dream, so be gone." Fear and dread twisted inside him. "Answer me. I have a right to know what's going on!"

"You have come to my door," a voice drooled out each word. "A gate of sorts between the last semblance of life, and the first step into… buurup… me."

Thomas turned around in panic, searching for another possible source for the voice, but saw nothing except that dark blotch in the fog. "Show yourself! I will not fall for some Halloween prank."

The smudge drifted closer. The darkness, gaining definition, appeared to be more like an ominous cave or black hole.

"Be gone, I want nothing to do with you," stammered Thomas.

A gurgling sound came from the direction of the hole, the sound twisting around Thomas. The darkness grew bigger, but with only grayness with which to compare, he couldn't be sure. Thomas stumbled a few steps away from the hole fighting to control his rising panic.

"You're an evil thing, and… Please, go away… NOW!" shouted Thomas.

The darkness moved with him. Again it belched out a foul odor, making Thomas gag. The smell clawed at his soul, catching each breath with angst. He swallowed to tamp down his nausea, as fear pulsed throughout his body.

"What are you doing? Get away from me."

The hole continued to move with Thomas.

It wants me... Nooo, is it coming for me? The stench pushed his terror to unbearable proportions. Fear thrashed about in Thomas' mind, trying to get out.

A strange thought pushed its way into Thomas. *Step into the darkness, don't fight it... just let yourself become part of it. That's the way to triumph over fear—become part of it.*

"Ech!... I can't... I can't breathe," Thomas gasped.

Panic gripped his soul, and he tried to run. With no bearings, he fell multiple times, gravel digging into his knees and palms; ignoring the pain, Thomas rolled and kicked to get away. All the while, from over his shoulder, he heard the hole gurgle and belch.

"Fool… there is nowhere to go, for you belong to me. Why fight the inevitable?" taunted the black hole.

"Be gone! You're evil and I want no part of you." Thomas scrambled and stumbled, landing this time on his bottom. Pushing with his legs and hands, he scooted backward. "Someone, please help me… I need help!"

A barely perceptible shift in the grayness occurred, moving to lighter shades, and with it the gurgling drifted further into the grayness. Off to the side, a faint glow appeared like a light in the fog. To Thomas's great relief, the awful smell also began to recede and his breathing became easier.

"Light!" He breathed it in. With great effort, Thomas rose to his feet and moved toward the glow, wheezing and coughing up dark plugs of mucus with each step. "I need light. Please, stop the darkness from getting me!"

As Thomas staggered toward the light, his fear of the black hole receded, but with each step, a new problem arose. The light became stronger and began to hurt his eyes. In the brilliance Thomas had to squint to make out the faint outline of three people gathered at the feet of the source of the blinding luminescence.

"It's so beautiful," he whispered. "I want to be there to bask in the light."

After a few steps, his skin began to tighten with heat to the point of rupturing like molten lava. He stopped, worried that another step would bring his destruction, and looked down at himself to see what caused such scorching pain. "What? My skin!" It had shriveled and begun to split. To his horror, his hands and arms were covered with red-orange sores, belching out small puffs of smoke. The odor of rotting fish drifted up from his body and made him choke.

"Hey, what's going on?" He tried to cry out, but his tongue and throat stuck for lack of moisture, and only a garbled sound came forth.

Strangely, the light drew his attention from himself back to its beauty, like a wondrous sunrise lighting up the entire sky. Thomas longed to draw as close to the source as possible, and he once again pushed forward. With each step the light became brighter, and the burning of his skin grew in intensity. The light now caused the fissures on his arms to open and bubble a foul reddish goo.

A horrible fact occurred to Thomas, *I can't get any closer to the light for the heat will burn me up with its brilliance. But if I turn back to save myself, I will be swallowed by the dark hole, never to see light again.* The horror of his situation came down on Thomas like a crushing weight, sinking him to his knees in agony.

"You can't survive there," came a gurgling voice from behind. "They don't care about you; you are nothing to them. Give up; it's hopeless. Come, take your place in me; I am far better than being burned to death. Stop fooling yourself, you'll never be able to join the light because you look more like me than it. Come join your own kind in my shadows."

"No… no, I don't want darkness; I need light," Thomas screamed. "If only I could join those who sit at the feet of the glorious radiance, to be able to drink in the beauty, to be surrounded by peace and share their joy."

"Peace? Joy? They won't get you what you really want. What you've secretly desired since starting in research… the Nobel Prize." The tenor of the voice changed to a more formal one, filled with wisdom and authority. "We have lots of great scientists here. They gather often to exchange ideas and awards. The light doesn't care about your intelligence! Why that place wants you to deny yourself, your greatness, your intellect. With me you get to keep all of your awards and honors, the very things you've worked so hard to achieve—self is king here, not there." The hole oozed a little closer to Thomas, being careful to stay in the shadows.

The light's intensity grew, causing the dark hole to stop and retreat. The radiance scorched the black hole, causing its edges to curl and crack like sun baked mud. With a snarl it fell back into the grayness. As it pulled away, the hole called out a warning, "The light will only burn you up. You will never be able to live in its light. Why be in agony when you can have all the pleasures of the world in me."

Thomas in agony turned to the light and let out a sigh, he envied the three figures gathered before the source of all beauty. The radiance glowed with peace, joy, love, and many other colors that Thomas lacked the words to describe.

If I could only have a part of what they have, thought Thomas as he shielded his eyes from the intensity. *So close yet so far away. One small drop of what they have would keep that dark hole away and give my life goodness.* He staggered to his feet and attempted to take another step toward the light but fell once more to his knees.

"Please," Thomas implored. "Let me come into the light."

"No one is stopping you," boomed the light.

The sound nearly crushed Thomas. He struggled to get up, but the blinding brightness made him stop and fall back again.

"Ow, it is too bright!" he screamed, closing his eyes, but the searing light did not diminish. Thomas cried out, "Help me! I cannot draw closer because the light is too fierce. But I can't fall back, for the darkness will swallow what is left of my life. I am caught in between with no way to go! Please, won't you help me?"

"The darkness claims you because you have chosen it over Me." The words shook Thomas like thunder.

"Chose?" protested Thomas. "The dark hole chokes me with its foul stench, and I can't breathe. Yet your radiance burns me up so that I cannot come close. What choice do I have?"

"The glory of this land is too much for you. You ignored it while on earth, thus standing in the presence of true glory is more than you can bear."

"Is there nothing for me?" Thomas winced, for the glory the before him uncovered the truth of his life. The judgement of not being able to come to the light brought a dreadful sadness like someone dying of thirst seeing water that they cannot reach. "I beg you to send one of those in Your presence with just a drop of what you have to soothe my dry throat and withered soul. Let them help me… please!"

Thomas began to be overwhelmed by burning in every part of his body. Finally, he had to shove himself back because of the pain and heat. At the same moment, a gurgling came from behind and brought with it the dreadful scent of hopelessness. Thomas dared not to look back, afraid of what waited ready to swallow him in its darkness, forever lost to light. *What should I do? If I step back further, it will take me, but I can't stand here—the glory burns with each breath.* In desperation Thomas began to wail, "Have mercy, please, I beg for mercy!"

Chapter 3 - Joshua

"Blessed are the poor in spirit, for theirs is the kingdom of heaven." Matthew 5:3

Meeting Joshua

Ever so slightly a cool wind stirred, the burning eased, and Thomas could breathe again. Along with the refreshing breeze, Thomas thought he heard singing in the distance.

Be strong ye people in His might
He gives us courage in the fight.
The battle belongs to the Lord.
By God's grace, the battle's been won,
Even though it's just begun.
The battle belongs to the Lord.
In all things to Jesus you must avail
For by His blood we will prevail.
The battle belongs to the Lord.

Lifting himself, Thomas turned to see who brought him such wonderful relief. Straight ahead, some distance off, a man walked toward Thomas. As he came closer, Thomas wondered at the powerful greatness of this being. He stood at least six feet tall (but seemed much taller), dressed in dazzling armor of gold and silver. In his hand he held a sword that shown even brighter than the armor. Thomas had to squint to even look at him. Such grandeur went far beyond anything Thomas had ever known. *This must be a king or highly regarded knight of heaven coming to my rescue.* Though the knight's regal bearing and obvious strength impressed Thomas, it was his smiling face that commanded attention. Like the smile of a child, it brought joy to all who gazed upon its dazzling goodness. Thomas couldn't help but fall back a few steps, ashamed of how his own appearance must appear to this glorious being before him.

"Stop! Don't pull back," said the man. "If you move toward the darkness trying to hide from your shame, you will fall over the edge. Just give yourself some time and your eyes will become accustomed to my presence. My name is Joshua. The light of the world sent me to assist you; I certainly don't want my arrival to be the cause of your death."

At Joshua's warning, Thomas froze. The thought of falling into the black hole brought up visions of horror. Immediately he fell to the ground grasping the rocks, his mind seized with fear at what evil lingered for him somewhere in the grayness.

"Please, don't let me fall into that hole!" Thomas begged.

"No one accidentally falls into the dark pit," said Joshua. "It's a choice you make."

"That's what the radiant light said,… but it burns! Even your presence makes me worried I might burn up. How can I choose the light? Its brilliance burns and forces me away," Thomas shuddered. "There is no choice. For the light I desire I cannot bear, but moving away to protect myself takes me into the darkness."

"Oh, but you've been choosing your entire life," said Joshua.

"But I tried moving toward the light and couldn't, for the radiance blinded me and scorched my skin," Thomas protested. Suddenly, he remembered the ugliness of his arms and hands in the light and haltingly looked down. His open sores were much smaller, but his skin looked cracked and ghostly gray.

"Your appearance only reflects what you long for—what you treasure."

"You accuse me of wanting to be like this," objected Thomas. "Who would want to be excluded from the light? Tell me when did I choose between glory and decay? Please, don't leave me in this state. Now that I've glimpsed the holy, tell me how can I join you? I want what you have."

Joshua gazed at Thomas, "You've ignored heaven's overtures in the past, choosing instead your own way. Why would you want to be different now?"

"Because now I know what is true magnificence. I want to be like you—clothed in glory. I want to see the beauty you gaze upon. I want to sit in the presence of the light without burning up. I want to drink in heaven's goodness."

"'I want' consumed your life on earth with seeking temporal things for yourself. Now that you understand what real glory is, you think you can obtain it with earthly avarice. What good is it if you gain the whole world but in the process miss out on life? Honestly, there is not much life left in you."

"I beg you, please!" pleaded Thomas. "It is agony to see that such beauty exists and not be able to partake in it. Tell me, what is it that allows you to rest in such glory yet keeps me from the same joy?"

"A life lived ignoring the eternal, atrophies in its ability to stand before true joy. You can't stop looking at yourself and comparing what you have to what you see in others. Instead of rejoicing at seeing God's glory reflected in them, you covet it."

"Isn't heaven delighted that my skill saves lives?" Thomas protested. "I'm a hero to so many people. How can you say I've failed to develop the ability to appreciate joy? I should be honored in heaven, not this." Thomas grew sullen looking at his gray cracked skin.

"Your foolish words and pride are pushing you away from the truth. Come closer my friend, for I wish to show you what you have spent a lifetime missing." Joshua motioned with his hand for Thomas to step beside him.

Lord Have Mercy

As Thomas drew closer, he felt a refreshing coolness that permeated the air about Joshua. "I know you don't remember me, but I remember you," said Joshua with a smile. "How God weaves life into lives is amazing."

"But I am new to this place and you are the first person I have met. How can we have met before?" questioned Thomas

"O my, I didn't mean here between heaven and hell, but back on earth." laughed Joshua.

"Please, give me credit for some observational skills. Really, I think I could remember someone of your bearing and stature no matter where I might be."

"On earth you looked only upon the external person," pointed out Joshua. "Here it is all about the inner person reflecting the fullness of the Creator."

With the mention of earth, Thomas recalled gasping for breath then collapsing on the airplane. "No, no… I can't stay here, send me back. I have a dedication speech to give; they're going to name the research center after me. I have so much more left to do—my work. I am not ready to die!"

"Oh, but the truth is you've been dead for a long time," Joshua said with sadness. "You have ignored the light and joy of life, choosing instead to worship false gods." Then Joshua pointed to something lurking behind Thomas. "It's been waiting for you."

Without daring to look, Thomas froze when he heard the gurgling directly behind him. "No, please don't let it take me." Thomas pleaded. "I want to stay here with you, in the light, or send me back to my life on earth."

"Life… that is not mine to give or take. Instead, I have been sent to teach you. Now come with me," said Joshua. "You have much to learn. I am permitted to let you experience my existence on earth. Like you, I once misunderstood the gift of life, but by His mercy He healed my blindness. Hopefully, through my eyes, you will come to see and understand what true life is all about. I caution you that being in me will seem strange at first and not easy, but hang in there and seize this chance of grace. You will be living my life, seeing with my eyes, and even experience my thoughts and feelings, but because the scene is from what has already happened, you cannot influence or change anything. If it all becomes too much for you, and you need to pull back, just pray aloud—'LORD, have mercy,' and you will be back here."

Thomas laughed, "Lord, have mercy? That's what my grandma said whenever she caught me making a mess. 'Lawd have mercy' she would say."

Joshua laughed too as he put his hand upon Thomas. "She certainly is a beautiful lady."

"What? You know my grand…"

Whoosh.

Coming out of the dense fog, the gray dissipated and Thomas found himself sitting on an examination table covered by a strip of crinkly white paper. He had red shorts on but no shirt; his heart pounded with fear. Sticking out of the shorts were thin legs twitching with nervous energy. On his feet he wore scuffed up sneakers with velcro instead of laces and Superman socks.

I must be experiencing Joshua's life as a young child, thought Thomas. *How odd I can even feel his anxiety over being in a doctor's office.* Across the room a sink jutted out of the wall, and above it an eye chart with boats and planes in ever smaller lines. Overhead fluorescent lights gave everything a sterile blue feeling. Josh's eyes darted about the room like a bird looking for danger.

"I want to go, now," spoke Josh. "No shots, bad, bad."

Strange—Thomas experienced the words coming from his mouth, but not from him. He could feel and see everything like it was really happening to him, yet he only could observe. He couldn't make his arm move but felt the hand make a fist. Even more alarming, Thomas felt the rising anxiety and fear in Josh. Adding to the fear, the room smelled of alcohol swabs, triggering in Josh apprehension over getting a shot. He began looking for a way to escape. Next to the exam table stood a large lady talking to someone not in Josh's field of vision. Thomas knew it would be the doctor, but Josh thought it might be a monster coming to get him like in his dreams. A giant wave of angst surged in Josh; his legs bounced, his mind whirled with thoughts of needles and what unknown dark things would do to him. In fact, Thomas noted every part of Josh—muscle, skin, limbs, all twitching with fear.

"I get down, now." Josh's anxiety level climbed higher with each minute, making it impossible to sit still. The lady's hand grew more firm on Josh, squishing down to keep him on the exam table.

"Out!" said Josh. "I want to get out."

"Joshie, you sit still for the doctor while he examines you," said the woman. "With all your squirming, I can't hear what he's saying."

Thoughts of pain and fear continued to build in Josh. He knew the conversation concerned him, but he did not understand many of the words. Big words, strange words, words smelling of alcohol, words always led to horrible things happening—sharp things poking—causing pain.

"As I was saying," said the doctor. "The lab tests show no indication of a genetic problem, but my exam shows classic signs and symptoms of Fetal Alcohol Syndrome, along with profound relationship difficulties typical of Reactive Attachment Disorder."

"That figures," said the woman. "His mother drank during the pregnancy and used any drugs she could lay her hands on. The neighbors called 911 when they heard someone crying for hours. The police broke into the house and found Josh's mom passed out on the couch, and poor little Josh shut away in a closet. Who knows how long he had been locked up in the dark? In all my years of working for Child Protective Services, this is the worst case of neglect I have ever seen."

"That explains his growth retardation and some of his behavior problems," said the doctor. "It is hard to predict how much his condition will improve with time and what is permanent."

"I need to place him in a foster home but can't with him acting out like this," said the woman. "Isn't there anything more you can do to control his behavior?"

"We can clear up his skin sores and control the seizures, but the alcohol and emotional neglect may have damaged Josh beyond help. What a pitiful waste of life."

Josh didn't understand the big words, but an inner angry voice yelled, *broken... no good... bad*. This kept repeating in ever increasing volume.

Thomas reeled at the litany of bizarre ugly thoughts and feelings now flooding Josh. *I hate you... you're a monster... no one likes monsters... bad... bad, bad, bad!* Josh's fist started pounding on the side of his head as he yelled, "No Good, no good, NO GOOD!" The punches were not light taps to draw sympathy, but harsh hits meant to punish. Josh wanted release from all his stupidness, fear, and ugliness. If he couldn't pound it out, then he didn't care about living. Thomas worried about Josh's growing revulsion and felt that he might explode at any moment. This experience in Josh wasn't like reading about Fetal Alcohol Syndrome. He felt it, became part of it. He now understood why Josh used physical pain as a means to drown out the mental anguish and fear. Having been shut up alone in a closet, the dark scared him like nothing else.

Get out, get out, they're going to throw you in the black hole, Josh's mind vibrated with panic, escalating to the point that Thomas felt his own mind begin to explode. With his own panic rising with Josh's, Thomas cried out, "Lord, have mercy! I can't take this anymore."

Whoosh.

Instantly, Thomas found himself back in the gray mist with Joshua's reassuring hand on his shoulder. "I couldn't think! I felt overwhelmed by emotions that were running in ten directions at once," said Thomas looking up at Joshua. "The overwhelming fear of darkness, there must be some mistake. How could that be you?"

"It's no mistake. My earthly mind had severe problems from my mom's drinking and being neglected," remarked Joshua. "I may have looked like an unruly child from the outside, but the fear and anger raged far worse on the inside. I hated my life and feared anyone who touched me."

"But how could that be you? I mean, look at you now," Thomas said. "Nothing makes sense — ruled by fear with a dysfunctional brain. How could such a mess produce someone so glorious?"

"That is what I hope to show you; let me take you back," Joshua said again, reaching out to Thomas.

"No, wait, I don't know if I…"

Joshua touched Thomas' shoulder. "Ready or not…"

Whoosh.

"Josh, Josh! Settle down. Are you listening to me?" said the woman standing next to the exam table. She grabbed Josh's hand to stop him from pounding his head. Then she put her other hand on his shoulder and neck to calm him with gentle pressure.

"Get away; you're hurting me," yelled Josh. "No touching, no touching!" Josh became more agitated the more she tried to keep him still. Suddenly he reached up and dug his fingernails into the woman's hand.

"Ow! You hurt me," she screamed. "See doctor… his aggressive behavior. He fights with everyone, even hits himself. People are afraid of him—no one wants him, and it's only getting worse." The woman rubbed her hand. "There must be something more you can do?"

"Behavioral therapy may help him learn some control," said the doctor. "But with all the brain damage, I wouldn't give him much hope.

Josh's face started to burn. He turned to slide off the exam table and get away. That is when Thomas saw the name on the doctor's lab coat, Dr. Thomas Jones, Pediatrician, Chief of Genetics. Thomas wanted to look at the doctor's face to confirm this surreal experience of meeting himself, but Josh did not look up. He wanted to get away from whatever terrible thing they were about to do to him. The woman blocked his escape by moving to the foot of the exam table.

"Ennnnnnnnn," Josh clenched his teeth. His fear continued to build, fueled by gurgling thoughts from somewhere deep inside. *They're going to throw you back in that dark closet and leave you there forever. No one wants you... no good... dummy... stupid... an animal, that's what you are! Hate you, hate you,... HATE YOU.* Fear and self-loathing pounded through his mind — suffocating, Josh felt like he was drowning. That's when he started hitting himself again; yelling and cursing, "bad, bad, bad," using the self-inflicted pain to fend off the monster in his head.

"No Josh, you are not to hit yourself." The woman grabbed Josh's arms to keep him from pounding his head.

"Noooo! Get away," Josh yelled. He kicked hard, catching the woman in the hip.

"Ow, you little…" she whispered, as she clamped down harder.

"Bad, no good, BAD," growled Josh hitting his leg then fighting to get away. Josh exploded with nervous agitation that choked out all other thoughts. "Kill it, kill it. Bad, BAD, BAD!" he yelled. Then Josh started tearing at his clothes. They were hurting, feeling tight, suffocating. "I can't breathe! Get out, GET OUT!"

Dr. Jones reached over to pin Josh to the exam table and prevent him from falling. All the touching only escalated Josh's panic. "Noooo, get away!" All three of them thrashed about; that's when Josh bit the doctor.

"You little…this kid's a menace," cursed Dr. Jones as he pulled back, releasing Josh. Thrashing about, Josh fell off the table and hit his head on the floor. The lights blinked, and Josh seized.

Thomas had witnessed seizures and treated them, but never experienced one—bouncing lights, cramping muscles, not able to breathe, a panic of the mind and body that wouldn't stop. But the explosion of self-anger scared Thomas the most. "I can't stand this," Thomas called out. "Lord, have mercy!"

Whoosh.

Thomas found himself back in the gray fog, completely shaken by what he had just experienced. He looked up at Joshua.

"You're the child who bit me," Thomas said utterly dumfounded. "I remember... who could forget. The bite became infected; I almost lost my hand because of you. It took weeks to heal."

"Yes, I am the one who bit you. Please forgive me," said Joshua.

"But what?..." The experience continued to rattle Thomas. "You were an animal... severely damaged... dominated by fear, and anger. It's a wonder you could think at all. Why even being touched caused you pain. How could your pitiful messed up brain overcome all that?"

In response Joshua sang, "Oh, His right arm will triumph where all else fails. His power's not limited by the strength of man. Praise, honor and glory are His…"

Thomas ignored what he considered trite simplistic blathering and pressed on with his inquiry. "I was there: your thoughts were suffocating—you had to fight to keep from being overwhelmed by the fear of being alone in that dark closet. I could hear the darkness speak. It twisted your mind into knots. No one could survive such insanity, let alone become…"

Stopping his song, Joshua looked at Thomas. "At least you now know a little of why I hit and bit. Fetal Alcohol Syndrome and fear of being alone in that closet had distorted my view so much, I just saw you and everyone as enemies. My brain had been so scarred I hated it. I hated life; so I fought everything, but mostly myself. When you hate yourself—everything around you becomes a war zone."

"Yes, that's my point," interrupted Thomas. "It doesn't make sense… I mean look at… you're…"

"Glorious…I reflect God now, not myself." Joshua broke into a smile that spilled over on Thomas with joy.

"I don't see how you could go from a life of chaos, like I just experienced, to one filled with beauty, joy, and…" Thomas searched for words to describe Joshua. "It's a fairy tale that I just don't swallow. Your life meant nothing. You couldn't even think right, and now you are the reflection of God! How do you go from a useless life to one of kingly privilege, and I get left behind with nothing?"

"Yeah, pretty miraculous what God can do," beamed Joshua. "For God to take something so deformed by abuse and make it into…"

"But what about me?" protested Thomas. "I give my best to help people through medicine, and now look at me. Doesn't my life's work count for anything? Where is the justice in it all? Why does God award you, who has done nothing, with magnificence; and I, who has done brilliant things—nothing? After all the new treatments I discovered through genetics, the research building I helped finance, shouldn't I have been given at least some credit and glory for a life of such notable achievement?"

"In a hundred years, they will tear down that building and erect something else, rarely mentioning your name. In the light of eternity, it is all so small. All men are like grass, and all their glory is like the flowers of the field; the grass withers and the flowers fall, but the word of the Lord stands forever."

"You're saying that all the good I've done through my research is nothing?" defended Thomas.

"Scientific advancement is great," responded Joshua, "but all the glory men heap upon themselves about understanding DNA looks pretty small compared to the one who created DNA. Don't get stuck on rating and comparing the accomplishments of science, instead seek the approval from the source of all good things."

"But, you did nothing and got everything. It's not fair; there must be some mistake. I demand justice."

"Oh Thomas, you have justice, but what you need is mercy. There is still much for you to learn…"

"Don't 'Oh Thomas' me! I am not a child. You were the one with brain damage. I am the doctor here."

"Here? If you mean heaven, your earthly glory and my damaged brain mean nothing here. I am the recipient of grace just like everyone in heaven. What you see is the reflection of God's glory. None of it is mine. So even though you see me, it's really Him you marvel at."

"Then why can't I reflect His glory?" inquired Thomas. "It only seems to burn me."

"You sought and received the glory of earth for your work," said Joshua. "You reflect here what you sought there."

Thomas looked down at his dirt smudged clothes.

Joshua smiled and breathed out. "O Lord, open his eyes."

"How can someone have everything when they did nothing?" Thomas muttered to himself, "And my life amounts to nothing but dirty rags and oozing sores?"

Joshua looked carefully at Thomas. "I am afraid it is worse than nothing. You're slowly becoming a black hole, sucking everything to itself, unable to reflect anything good. That is the end you've been working toward."

Thomas froze at the mention of a black hole. "No! You're wrong, I'm a good person. Actually, I've done more than most…"

"Good in whose eyes?" questioned Joshua.

Thomas suddenly realized how self-centered that sounded. In his mind a picture formed of an astronomical "Black Hole," sucking up everything, even light into itself. His thoughts suddenly coalesced into the horrid black hole waiting in the mist. "Noooo," Thomas wailed, "I don't want that. Is there any hope of glory for me?" His thoughts collapsed inward, and he thought of the darkness of his own making. "Lord, have mercy!"

After a long spell battling his own fear of the dark, Thomas felt exhausted and looked again at Joshua. "How did you do it?" he sighed. "Is there any way for me to have what you have?"

"There is no formula or ritual… It's a gift of grace," responded Joshua. "That's the wonder of heaven. This glorious life doesn't depend on knowledge or achievement but on trusting in the one who is life. Jesus wants to share His glory with us and through us."

"I can't even look at his glory, let alone reflect it, without burning up. How do I trust what hurts me?" Thomas pondered his predicament. "The glory of God forces me to run away. If you had not come to my aid, I would have run off into darkness to escape what I could not bear."

"That is both the blessing and curse of this land," remarked Joshua. "The blessing is that here everything is exposed and completely known. The curse is there is nowhere to hide from the truth that you are lost, alone and spiritually bankrupt. The lamp of the Lord searches the spirit of man; it searches out his inmost being. Nothing can hide from His truth."

"Am I lost to any goodness?" Thomas trembled with this thought. "Please, is there any hope of light, of love and beauty, or am I forever left out?"

Joshua looked at Thomas with great pity. "That is not for me to decide. Come, there is more I must show you. This occurs later in my

life at a group home. I was seventeen at the time."
Joshua placed his hand again on Thomas.

Whoosh.

Alone/forsaken

"Josh, the police want to talk with you,"
said a voice from outside a closed bedroom door.
Josh sat on a twin bed in a room only slightly
bigger than the bed. The walls were covered with
posters of rock bands; rumpled under his feet a
small stained throw rug. An empty soda bottle lay
on its side next to his nightstand. A lava lamp,
digital clock, and an empty bag of pretzels sat
atop the stand. Josh quickly grabbed the bag and
soda bottle and threw them into the trashcan by
the bed. The crumbs he hurriedly brushed away
under the bed.

Knock, knock, knock…

"Josh! open this door now."

Josh opened the door a crack. "Yeah, what
do they want?"

"Open the door; they're here to discuss
something with you, Josh."

Thomas could see that the man at the door had a name tag above his shirt pocket: "Mike, Supervisor, Vista Group Home." Mike motioned with his hand and two uniformed police officers stepped into Josh's room.

"Josh, I can't believe we are here again," said the first officer. Josh just looked at the floor, filled with shame. Not because he had broken the rules, but because of not being smart enough to avoid getting caught. "This is the third time you stole pop and pretzels from the mini-mart. Give us what is left, and we'll return it."

Josh went over to his dresser. In the top drawer, hidden behind his socks, he pulled out three bottles of pop and two bags of pretzels. Under his breath he began to repeat, "bad, bad, bad…" The agitation and self-hate began to ramp up in Josh, emotions lashing out from somewhere deep. They were an ugly mixture of anger, self-loathing, and fear. Then, with no forewarning, they blew into a gale that knocked over all other thoughts. "Bad, bad, bad…" Josh wanted to hurt himself, inflict pain to quiet the storm raging in his head, but with the police present he remained stoic.

"I'm warning you Josh, soon you will be eighteen and considered an adult. If you keep this up, we'll throw you in jail. For now, you can no longer go into that mini-mart, or the owner is going to press charges." The policemen placed the items in a plastic shopping bag and left.

After Mike closed the front door, he returned to Josh's room. "Josh, you know the rules. You won't be able to stay here if you don't behave. Why would you go out and steal pop when you have some in the kitchen refrigerator?"

"I don't know; I don't remember nothing; it just happens. My head doesn't think right," Josh said, giving himself a quick cuff to the head.

Thomas could feel a vast emptiness in Josh's mind that hampered Josh from connecting his actions with right or wrong. Bad, stupid, hurt, ugly, and shame continued to swirl around like angry birds driving off any good thought.

"Bad, bad, bad…" said Josh trying to show Mike he understood and would be good in the future. Josh then began to hit himself up side of the head; punishment for a brain that didn't work right.

"JOSH! You are not to hit anyone, including yourself. Now stop it," scolded Mike. "To help you remember not to hit or steal, you have to stay here at the house tonight instead of going to the baseball game."

"Why can't I go?" pleaded Josh. There were two things Josh loved, motorcycles and baseball. He couldn't own a motorcycle, much less have the ability to ride it, and now he couldn't go to the baseball game.

"Josh, you just stole things from the mini-mart; you have to have some consequence."

"WHY?" whined Josh.

"That's just the way life is. You do wrong, and you get punished." Mike closed the bedroom door and left.

Josh sat on his bed and started to cry, "Bad, bad, bad," he said over and over, hitting his head harder because of no baseball.

Josh's feelings of rejection and self-loathing overwhelmed Thomas. He wondered how Josh had survived this life for so long. Accusations and shame kept pounding Josh's mind with: *you're a worthless lump of flesh... you'll never think right... you're no good for anything... you should have never been born.* Like a shroud of black oil, these thoughts began to cling to everything, and no amount of rubbing, cursing, or hitting could free Josh from their incessant drumming.

Thomas could barely withstand this barrage of ugly thoughts. Then it struck him—this vileness comes from the black hole… *Oh no, it must be nearby!* Fear whipped his mind, and the urge to run and call out "Lord, have mercy" surged in Thomas. *I must get out of here. Wait, Joshua survived this somehow; maybe that is what I am here to learn.* Thomas forced his mind to concentrate on observing and not running.

Josh cried into his pillow, intermittently hitting his head until he became exhausted and fell asleep. Soon a strange dream commenced in Josh's troubled mind. He stood in a large room with bars on the windows facing a large desk. Behind the desk sat a stern-faced Dr. Jones with a bandage on his hand, and to the side in a jury box sat the social worker, Mike the supervisor, and two strangers—a man and woman. In the audience sat a group of people scowling at Josh for no reason that Thomas could figure out.

Dr. Jones pounded the gavel at Josh. "You stand before this court accused of stealing, hitting and biting." Then turning to the jury "What is your verdict upon Josh for stealing?"

"Guilty," everyone said in unison.

"Your verdict on hitting?"

"Guilty."

"And your verdict for biting?" Dr. Jones asked as he held up his bandaged hand.

"Guilty!"

Then Dr. Jones turned toward the jury box and questioned, "Do you as his mother and father want Josh in your home?"

The man and woman immediately replied, "No, he is worthless. We got rid of him once, and we do not want him back—ever!"

"Do any of you foster parents want him?" Dr. Jones said, looking around the court.

"No!" came a loud chorus.

Dr. Jones turned to look at Josh, "The court agrees with the jury. You are responsible for all the pain and ugliness that has happened: Your mother and father leaving you; being kicked out of the foster homes for constantly fighting, kicking, and biting. You're a worthless lump of flesh… you'll never think right… you are good-for-nothing and bad beyond hope. You should have never been born. Therefore, you shall be taken from this court and placed in the black hole forever. Guards, throw him into the darkness and lock the door."

The guards grabbed Josh and wrestled him toward the dark hole at the back of the court-room. "Mine, you're mine," gurgled the cavity. As it spoke, a foul odor wafted through the court-room filling everyone with the stench of death.

"No, no, noooo!" screamed Josh. "I'm scared of the dark. Help me, someone please help me."

The guards tightened their grip as Josh fought to avoid the darkness. In one last heave, Josh tumbled into the blackness of the dark hole. Josh screamed as the darkness coated everything in its putrid ooze. The more Josh struggled to free himself, the deeper he sank in the slime.

Thomas knew it was only a nightmare, but seeing himself play the role of judge and speaking the horrible words against Joshua's life brought to mind the many times he had held disdain for people like Josh. This dream seemed too real. He gasped, feeling his own shame choke in his throat.

"I can't breathe, I can't breathe," gasped Josh.

"Wake up, wake up!" shouted Thomas, his own panic exploding in the suffocating darkness of Josh's mind. Josh awoke wrapped in his bed cover punching and kicking to get free. With one big punch, he hit the nightstand sending the lava lamp to the floor.

"Help me! Get me out of here!" Josh hollered.

The night supervisor, hearing the commotion, raced into the bedroom, "Josh, Josh wake up. You are having a nightmare."

But Josh kept kicking and screaming. Finally, the supervisor grabbed Josh, pinning his body to the bed.

"You're okay Josh; it's just a bad dream. Wake up."

"Let me go. Bad, bad, bad!" Josh cried, fighting the last vestiges of the dream. Suddenly his right arm broke free of the covers, and he gave himself a hard punch to the head, trying to drive out the fear. With that blow, Josh's eyes rolled back into a grand mal seizure and dreamless oblivion.

Thomas felt the seizure's jerking twitching force. This time he decided to try to ride out the seizure for the sake of his own curiosity. The awful buzz only intensified and began to pull Thomas under its spell of bouncing and jerking. That's when he noticed the squeezing around Josh's chest, not letting him catch his breath. The fear of dying mounted in Thomas until he couldn't take any more and yelled out, "I can't breathe, Lord, have mercy. Get me out!"

Whoosh.

Pulled back into the gray mist, Thomas fell to his knees, exhausted and reeling from the seizure. It took awhile for him to gather his scattered thoughts. Finally, he turned to Joshua. "Please don't take me into another seizure. I don't want to go through that again. Besides, it does nothing to help me understand."

"It is not the seizure," said Joshua, "but what put me into the seizure that you need to understand."

"You mean hitting your head?" questioned Thomas.

"One step before that. What made me punch myself?"

"I believe it would be hate," said Thomas. "I could feel it upwelling from inside; you hated yourself—a deep self-loathing!"

"That's evil's plan to get everyone thinking only of themselves," said Joshua. "In my case, I hated my dysfunctional brain—that's all I could think about. In your case evil's plan is to have you focus on success and all your achievements. Do you see this? When you're in the spotlight thinking only of yourself, you can't mirror anything else… it consumes the person you were created to be. That's what hell is—darkness reflected a thousand times until it is like black tar coating everything. It is the antithesis of heaven where all reflect the glory of God."

"But the darkness… it had you."

"Oh, it claims everyone, but many like yourself don't see it until they come here."

"Here?" asked Thomas.

"The gray lands, neither heaven nor hell. A place of judgement where hell comes to claim its own," replied Joshua.

"But I still don't understand," puzzled Thomas. "Your life reeked of hell, I have never known such horrid self-loathing and twisted thinking. Yet here you are the glory of heaven. But my life was good and filled with purpose… this whole exercise seems to be dragging me closer to darkness than to light. I don't want to do this anymore," Thomas shook his head, for he could feel the black hole stalking him and Josh's dream made it all too real. I want to return to my life, to finish what I started, to show I belong in heaven."

"You spent your life avoiding the truth about heaven and hell, blinding yourself with personal achievements. You need to return to my harsh life to give you clarity as to the ways and power of heaven." Joshua said, reaching out to put his hand on Thomas.

Wait! I…

Thomas grabbed Joshua's hand to push it away. As their hands touched his eyes rolled back, and he gasped.

Whoosh.

Choosing to Die

Thomas returned to the Josh's room as Josh struggled to grasp consciousness following the seizure. He lay sprawled on the floor, each muscle in his body ached and sagged with exhaustion. Scrambled is the only word to describe Josh's thoughts and feelings.

"Whaaaat is going on?" Josh's mind roused in spits and sputters. Coming out of the seizure, even the most basic thoughts swirled in pools of confusion. At first Josh had no memory of past events to reference his present, then bits and pieces began popping up, and the puzzle of who, what and where, concerning himself started to take shape. The harsh reality of having had a seizure dawned on him along with the misery of his defective brain being the cause. His thoughts further coalesced into feelings of shame and anger about his stupid Fetal Alcohol Syndrome. *I've messed up my brain. That makes me have seizures. I'm a worthless... I can't think right... I can't act right... I hate myself... I'm no good.* The body is the last to wake up. Piecing together how to move hands and legs, sensations of hot and cold, awareness of sounds, things touching the skin, and the sense of smell. For Josh this brought more shame when the stink of losing control of bowel and bladder clung to him. *Bad... bad... bad... stupid... stupid... stupid... worthless... worthless... worthless.* Accusations reverberated through his mind and soul.

"Josh, wake up. We need to get you changed and washed up," Mike said, trying not to gag. "You had another seizure." Mike had seen Josh go through seizures before. He and the night attendant had laid out a plastic drop cloth on which they wanted Josh to strip down. Then they would move him to the shower, if he could stand.

Josh followed orders, his mind too groggy to resist. As the shame of what had happened dawned on Josh, he took some of his excrement and smeared it on his chest.

"Josh, what are you doing? No!" Mike yelled, grabbing Josh's arm.

Josh looked at Mike and the night attendant. They had on surgical masks, blue paper hazardous material aprons, and plastic gloves for protection. All the fight had gone out of Josh. Mechanically, he followed Mike's orders. Josh had given up. A sullenness seeped through Josh and covered him with a heavy and suffocating sense of deadness.

After getting cleaned up, Josh slumped down at the breakfast table. Thomas noted that the normal anger and fight had left Josh, replaced by a dry flatness.

"Get your coat, Josh. It is time for you to go to work."

Josh walked to the group home van and sat in the back without saying a word. The van made its rounds, stopping at the various work sites for the group home members. Josh washed dishes at the assisted care apartments down by the river.

"Okay, I'll be back to pick you up at the end of your shift," the van driver said, as Josh got off. Josh turned and watched the van disappear across the bridge.

Instead of going in to work, he walked toward the river. Josh enjoyed seeing the water flow; it had a soothing effect. That's what he needed this morning, something to relieve him of the aching void that plagued his thoughts.

When Josh reached the apex of the bridge, he stopped and leaned over the railing contemplating the water rippling down below. Thomas became aware of faint voices welling up in Josh. "Go ahead jump; you have nothing to lose… It will be better than the life you have now… No one cares… You hate your life… End the pain and be free."

As if in a trance, Josh threw one leg then the other over the railing. He leaned forward facing the flowing water, his hands held tightly to the upper rail. The allure of death called to Josh, "Come on, just let go. In a blink it will all be over. You'll see, it will be so much better." With his arms shaking, Josh wondered why life's ultimate choice frightened him—he hated being stupid, that his brain didn't work right. No one wanted something broken; no girl would ever love him. No future, no hope, no nothing. His grip loosened a little. Life, love, family, for these his heart ached. Again the inner voice welled up, "You'll never be anything because you're too dumb!"

Thomas knew the conflict that raged in Josh. His own appeals joined the fray. *Don't do it.*

You can hold out… This can't be how your life ends… What about reflecting God's glory? Josh leaned out a little further. A stillness came over Josh, and he let go. Pitching forward and down, Josh looked and saw an ugly blackness below waiting for him. "Noooo," Josh and Thomas screamed together.

I don't want to die! flashed through Josh. "Help me, please God help me! I don't want to fall into the black hole. I'm afraid of the dark!" Josh prayed as he fell.

In that moment, panic gripped Thomas too, as he plunged with Josh. Thomas saw death waiting below in the water, dark, lifeless, merciless, licking its lips. Thomas called out with Josh. "Lord, have mercy."

Whoosh.

Learning to Trust

Back in the grayness, Thomas quickly turned to find Joshua.

"You killed yourself?" Thomas looked stunned and uncomprehending.

"Well, I tried, but by the grace of God I did not succeed," said Joshua.

"How?" asked Thomas. "You jumped."

"God answered my prayer and saved me from the dark abyss that waited for me." Golden tears of gratitude formed in Joshua's eyes, but before they trickled very far, they changed into butterflies and flew off in the wondrous light that spilled over Joshua. Overcome by the moment, Joshua spoke:

> A miraculous gift, salvation's net,
> Before my foes, a feast was set.
> New life arising from Christ's horrid death,
> Purest air where I had no breath.
> He brings forth food in the driest land,
> Hope gushes from the desert sand.
> His love squelching the accuser's threats,
> Forgiveness silencing my life's regrets.
> He wrangles glory from my disgrace,
> Victory when I've lost the race.
> He gives me light to replace my fears,
> Butterflies arising from my tears.

At this Joshua became quite emotional over the miracle in his life and turned toward the light that now bathed him and looked far off. Thomas could not see what held Joshua's attention, but he marveled at the radiance it produced in Joshua. Soon a song poured forth from Joshua:

"Great is Thy faithfulness, O God my Father,

There is no shadow of turning with Thee,

Thou changest not, Thy compassions they fail not..."

As the music floated, the gray mist seemed to brighten, so that Thomas had to bow his head and close his eyes. When Joshua finished the song, he reached out and lifted Thomas' head and looked into his eyes. With deep concern, Joshua spoke. "You spent your life devoted to science and fighting disease, but it is God's faithfulness and mercy that saved my life. It is time to return to that bridge and see the wonderful grace of God." He held Thomas by the shoulders, and with tears, bowed his head in prayer. "Lord, thank You for your mercy to me. May Thomas now see your grace in all its glory."

Whoosh…Thomas felt himself falling.

Smack! Josh hit the icy water and immediately started flailing his arms, trying to get a breath. "Lord, help me, I can't swim." Josh sucked in some water and panicked, flailing his arms.

"Put your feet down." Came a voice from shore. "You don't want to drown in four feet of water." A hand reached out and grabbed Josh by the collar and pulled him to shore. Cough, cough, wheeze, cough. Joshua struggled to breathe. The stranger hit him on the back a few times, causing Josh to cough up water, and his breathing eased.

"God must really think you are special for you to have survived that fall from the bridge. That's a long ways down, and the water is not deep, with boulders everywhere."

"I didn't fall; I… I jumped." Josh looked down in shame.

"As I was saying, you're pretty special," said the man who had pulled Josh from the water.

"Why do you say that? You don't even know me. Are you making fun of me?" Josh's hands tightened into fists as shame and anger welled up.

"What I speak is true," said the man. "The anger and shame you feel about yourself is the lie. There is a verse in the Bible just for you: 'Blessed are the poor in spirit, for theirs is the kingdom of heaven.' That's why you are special, because you are poor in spirit. And if you are special to God the Father, you are a special friend to me."

Josh looked carefully at the stranger. No one had ever told him he was a special friend in such an affirming manner. Usually special meant— —not quite right.

"Come, I caught some fish, and they're cooking at my camp in those trees. You can dry your clothes at my fire while we eat." When they got to the trees, Josh caught the scent of the fire and fish frying in butter.

"Mmmm, it sure smells good," said Josh, his hunger now aroused. As they broke through the brush into the camp, Josh's eyes grew wide in amazement. The clearing had a small fire, a black pan with fish frying, and a little one-man tent. But what really made Josh's heart skip—a gor- geous custom motorcycle. "Ooooo," exclaimed

Josh. The bike dazzled with chrome; even the engine sparkled. The body and fenders shined, painted metallic sky blue with white wings spanning the gas tank. Walking over to the bike, Josh carefully reached out to touch it, but then stopped and looked at the stranger to make sure he did not mind.

"Go ahead, you can touch it, and when your britches are dry, you can sit on it." The stranger's warm smile spread over Josh. "In the meantime, why don't you take off your wet shirt and put on my bike jacket. You look a little cold." The stranger held out his black leather biker's jacket. Josh nearly ripped the buttons of his shirt with excitement. The coat fit perfectly. Josh turned looking at himself, wanting this moment to last forever. "Sit, my friend, so I can serve you some food." The stranger lifted the skillet and nudged one fish onto a paper plate, then broke off a piece of bread and placed it next to the fish. Lifting it up he said, "Thank you Lord for this food and for saving my new friend." The man then gave the plate to Josh, who sat stunned at all that was happening. "What is your name?" asked the man.

"Josh."

"Josh, why were you jumping off the bridge?"

"I'm no good to anyone. My brain is bad, and I can't think right."

"So why did you call out for help?"

"Because the black hole wanted to swallow me, and I didn't want it to get me. I just wanted to be done with my life," bemoaned Josh. He looked at the dirt and pushed it with his foot. "It is one gigantic mess, and people hate me 'cause I'm stupid."

"I know for a fact that God saved you from killing yourself because He loves you and wants you to be His."

Josh looked up puzzled, "How do you know that?"

"You didn't die out there, and I pulled you out. Trust me… God loves you."

"I don't trust people much, and I don't like to be touched."

"So why did you take my hand and allow me to pull you from the river?"

"I needed help, I guess," said Josh in a whisper.

"Then let me give you more help. You like being warmed by the heat from the fire; it keeps you from freezing. Trusting God is like that. The world can be very cold and wet, but trusting God warms you up and makes life worth living."

"But why did God let this happen to me? I can't think right, and no one wants me. Not even my mother and father."

"You may not understand all the whys in life. After all, no one is as smart as God. But I know without a doubt God loves you," said the man, looking Josh in the eyes. "You can trust me on that."

"I'm not very smart, that's my problem," mumbled Josh. "My mind is bad and gets me into trouble. I hate it. That is why I jumped. I am nothing."

"Who in all the world can trust God more than someone who has nothing else to put their trust in? Trusting God with your nothing is what pleases Him."

"But I can't remember to be good. I can't figure things out. I can't do anything right. I am worthless."

"The Lord Almighty doesn't care what you can or can't do. He wants you to depend on Him. I mean, really, what can anyone do for God?"

"Yeah, that is kind of funny. People thinking they can do something for God." Josh laughed to himself.

"That is why you have to come to God by faith. That is really all anyone can do. When you place your trust in Jesus, this pleases God, and if God is pleased with you, then what else is there?"

"But I am a total reject..."

"Does this sound like your life? 'He was despised and rejected by men, a man of sorrows and familiar with suffering. Like one from whom men hide their faces...'"

"That's me all right," said Josh. "People see me coming and hide."

"It was written long ago, about Jesus. The Lord knows your pain and came to take the hurt upon Himself."

"I don't get it."

"By believing in Jesus, you receive God's love and give Him your pain."

"How do I know he'll take it?" said Josh.

"Because God's love for you made Jesus suffer and die for you, and then God raised Him from the dead as proof that He has taken care of all your pain. You just need to give it to Him and believe in His power over death."

"I just don't know; I want to believe, but…" Josh stared at his feet.

The man looked intently at Josh. "You know how much rejection hurts. Don't add to His pain by rejecting His love for you."

"I guess if God will be happy by my trusting Him, then at least I can make someone happy."

"Joshua, I am so pleased."

It startled Josh to hear someone call him Joshua. It made him feel important, a real somebody, but most of all it made him feel wanted.

Then with a joyous laugh the man hugged Joshua. "You are His child forever," the stranger said.

A strange feeling surged through Joshua, for touching usually made him anxious and frightened, but this time he felt something new and… and glorious.

"I want to give you a note so you won't forget," said the man. He quickly wrote on some paper, stuffed it in an envelope, and held it out to Joshua.

"I can't read good," Joshua said feeling embarrassed.

"That's okay, take it anyway," said the man as he shoved the paper in Joshua's pocket.

After the meal, the stranger took Joshua for a brief ride. Returning to the campfire, they both talked about baseball.

Suddenly, Joshua heard a rumbling on the bridge. He looked up and saw the van crossing over the river. "My ride! If I miss it, I'll be in big trouble." He quickly turned to the stranger, and said, "Thanks for the meal and for helping me," and off he ran.

Out of breath, Joshua boarded the bus and took a seat in the back. As the van crossed the bridge, he looked for the campsite to wave good-bye to the stranger. *Where did it go? It should be down there in that clump of trees.* Joshua thought hard, *Could I have been dreaming?* He quickly reviewed all that had taken place. *I jumped from the bridge… hit the water. Maybe I knocked myself out and just thought it all up.* That's when he noticed he still had on the motorcycle jacket. *I forgot to give it back. Now I am in for it. They'll think I stole it!* Sitting in the bouncing van, Joshua started to get anxious about being accused of stealing. *Mike told me if I stole one more thing, they would kick me out. I will have no place to go. Bad... bad.* Something in his mind spooked him. *Get rid of it before you're caught.*

He took the coat off, thinking to throw it out the window. That's when Joshua looked at the back of the jacket. The top rocker had some words. Struggling hard to make sense of the letters, Josh said out loud, "J-uus-tiif-ied by Faaa-iith," below the arching words a white cross blazed with "Saavv-ved by Y-E-S-H-U-A," and the bottom rocker had in gold, "H-is chiiilld for-evvver." He ran his finger over each word. Joshua felt a shiver run through him. That's when he re-membered he had forgotten his wet shirt back at the camp. Out of nowhere a thought popped to the front of Josh's mind, *He took my wet shirt and gave me his jacket—we traded. Yes, yes, the man called me Joshua. I am not Josh anymore. I trust Yeshua. I am His.* This wonderful thought ran over and over in Joshua's mind as he gently touched the leather coat, examining every inch. Finally tracing his finger again over the words, "His child forever." Joshua put the jacket back on and wrapped his arms about himself. "I belong to Yeshua," he sighed.

Peace and joy spread through Joshua. It pushed aside the sorrow and sadness. It amazed Thomas hearing these words echo in every part of Joshua—*His child forever… His child forever…* Whereas before Josh's mind seemed a vast wasteland of self contempt; it now overflowed with the joy and peace belonging to a loving family.

Oh, to stay in this moment forever, thought Thomas. As much as Joshua's life before made Thomas want to get away, the warmth of this moment made him want to stay and rejoice— "Lord, have mercy."

Whoosh.

Living to Learn

After this last experience in Joshua's life, returning to the gray lands seemed even more dreary. The gray mist grew thicker and darker, making breathing more difficult than Thomas remembered. The gray lands also had a peculiar effect on everything, siphoning off color and texture. It even faded the past, making remembrances appear lackluster and meaningless, diluting the miraculous into something tepid and easily dismissed.

"Joshua," called out Thomas, worried he might be alone in the ever thickening fog. "Are you still here?"

"Yes, Thomas, I am here."

"That was just a dream you had, right?...I mean Yeshua really didn't come Himself and save you? I mean it is a bit of a stretch for me to believe Yeshua would come personally to save you then give you His coat."

"If the Creator of all things came and died for me two thousand years ago, don't you think He would come at my moment of most need and pull me back from death?"

"I just don't think Jesus would intervene like that," said Thomas.

"Yeshua told the story of the shepherd who leaves the 99 to go out and find the one sheep who was lost. I was lost, and Yeshua my shepherd came just for me. Why is it so hard to believe?

Thomas struggled to keep alive the experience he had witnessed in Joshua's life. The mist seemed to dull the reality of Joshua's joyous faith and cast doubt on the validity of the words on his leather coat. Battling through the fog, Thomas called out, "Joshua help me, I am losing the clarity of the joy Yeshua brought to your life. I want to believe, but I can't help wondering that maybe this is all just a dream, brought on by my collapse getting off the plane…You know some trick my oxygen deprived mind is playing on me."

"It's called doubt," said Joshua. "One of the main tricks the black hole uses in combating heaven's light."

"I know I witnessed something extraordinary." Thomas wrestled with his doubts. "I saw the amazing glory of you becoming a child of God. Yet now the scene grows faint, slipping into the grayness. How do I hold on to it?"

"You can't rely on someone else's faith or experience. Trusting God and becoming His child is something you must do for yourself. Then follow Jesus in all your ways, like a child trusts their parents, even when you don't know the reason why."

"Trust?" sighed Thomas. "The only thing I could trust with my dad is that I'd never be good enough. Never quite measure up."

"The first step is to trust that God loves you and will always be faithful to love you regardless of what happens. Even then, do not be surprised when hell's scavengers try to tear down your faith. You must hold firm and have faith in His unchanging love for you."

"Wait a minute, you were a wild neglected kid; your pitiful mind wrecked by Fetal Alcohol Syndrome. Where is God's love in that? You go from utter chaos to peacefully sitting at Yeshua's feet simply by saying, 'I am God's child?' This all sounds too fantastic to be believable. I just don't buy it."

"Hey, you experienced what took place," protested Joshua. "It wasn't by my effort. It was Yeshua's doing."

The name Yeshua pushed back the fog clouding around Thomas. Joshua's face smiled with the goodness of heaven.

"There is power in the name Yeshua," said Joshua. The fog continued to back off.

"Is Yeshua the one whom you reflect?" asked Thomas.

"By God's grace, yes. Yeshua is Hebrew for God saves, and the name Joshua is a reflection of His name," responded Joshua. Light cascaded around them.

"So the coat and letter came directly from God?" Thomas struggled to wrap his mind around this miracle.

"Yes, but I didn't know it at the time," said Joshua.

"How come back there Yeshua looked so ordinary, but here I can't bear to be in His presence?"

"Jesus stooped down to find and rescue me. I still had to learn to trust Him before I could glimpse Him in all His glory. You, on the other hand, never learned the ways of faith, so you viewed me and Yeshua as not worth your time. When you don't know Him in love on earth, then when you get to this gray land, you see Yeshua as a fearful judge and run from Him," explained Joshua.

"I may not have been as devout as some," said Thomas, "but I would count myself as a Christian. Isn't that what faith is about?"

"Come, there is more to learn about trusting in the one who is faithful and true." Joshua again reached out and laid his hand on Thomas.

Whoosh.

Thomas felt the bounce of the van as it pulled into the driveway of Vista Group Home. Joshua quickly got off and tried to walk unnoticed to his room. Unfortunately, Robert, another client at the group home, spied Joshua running up the stairs in wet muddy shoes. "Hey, Josh, you're tracking mud in the house. Mike is not going to like that," Robert yelled so the entire house could hear. Mike looked up from the table he had covered with paperwork. Seeing the tracks from wet shoes, he got up and followed them to Josh's room.

Knock… knock "Josh, open the door. You have tracked mud in the house, and you must clean it up, but first we need to talk." Slowly the

door opened. "May I come in?" asked Mike.
Joshua nodded his head.

Thomas could feel the mounting anxiety in
Joshua—his jaw clenched, thoughts of wanting to
run away, and his hands tightening into fists.

"Josh where have you been?" asked Mike.
"Work called to say you didn't show up, and look
at your pants. They're all wet and muddy, like
your shoes." That's when Mike noticed the motorcycle jacket. "Where did you get that jacket,
Josh?"

Normally when Josh felt caught in something he knew to be wrong, he would look down,
avoid eye contact, and not answer. But this time,
he stared at the motorcycle jacket and a thought
popped into his consciousness—*trust God.*

"I jumped," Joshua blurted out.

"What does that have to do with this jacket?" Mike persisted.

"The man saved me and pulled me out of
the water. He took my dirty shirt and gave me
this…"

"Josh, are you telling the truth?"

"Yes, the man gave me the jacket. You can't
take it away. It is mine and…" Joshua hesitated,

wondering if Mike would believe him. "It's mine, and I am God's child forever. See, it says it right there." Joshua took the coat off and pointed at the back of the jacket. "And he gave me a new name. From now on I am Joshua. It means God saves. He told me so, and I… I believe him."

"That coat looks expensive. Are you sure he gave it to you? Maybe he is just letting you borrow it."

"No, He told me God loved me and saved me from dying in the river. He said I should trust God with my whole life, and I did. And it made the man happy. Then he gave me this jacket and took my wet shirt."

"Josh… I mean Joshua, let's find this person, so we can be sure he gave it to you."

They both got in Mike's car and drove to the bridge. Joshua pointed to the road on the far side that led down to the river's edge. Mike parked the car by the bank and they both walked into the clump of trees to find the campsite.

"There doesn't seem to be anyone here," said Mike. "Are you sure this is the place?"

"I don't know where he is, but he gave me the coat. I am God's child. He doesn't want me to lie anymore; I need to trust Him," Joshua said, trying to hold back his tears. "Please God, show Mike I'm telling the truth."

They looked around, but there was no campsite, no evidence of a fire, nothing to support Joshua's story.

"Josh, you want to tell me what really happened?"

"I told you, I'm not lying. I trust God now," said Joshua. His voice started to tighten.

Mike spotted something hanging from one of the trees. "Here is your shirt," he said, pushing through the brush. Holding it up, Mike noticed something written with charcoal on the back of the shirt. He read it out loud "Walk by faith," Followed by a cross and the words, "In Yeshua's love," Mike finished the reading with "My coat for Joshua's shirt… forever."

"See, I told you," said Joshua, hoping now Mike would believe him.

"How do I know you didn't do this yourself to hide the truth?" asked Mike.

The words crushed Joshua, and tears of frustration rolled down his cheeks. "But it is true! The man gave me the coat; you must believe me.

He wrote this, not me. I'm not smart enough to do this by myself."

Old patterns of negativity started bubbling up in Joshua. *No one believes a liar, It's all a lie… no one wants you. Bad… bad…*

"STOP…" A voice rolled through Josh that Mike could not hear, but rattled Thomas. "You are Joshua. The Lord Almighty, whose name you bear, loves you with an unfailing love." At this pronouncement the turmoil going on in Joshua stopped and fell back, and only one thought remained in Joshua—*I'm God's child.*

Joshua lifted his head and looked at Mike through tears, "I am God's child. I trust Him. This coat was given to me. I am telling the truth. You can't take the coat. It's mine. He gave it to me."

Mike looked at Joshua, "Give me the coat. I'll keep it until we can figure out who it belongs to."

A battle raged in Joshua. *Hit Mike, he is stealing your coat. You can't let him do that!*

The voice resounded again in Joshua, "Trust me; you are My child forever, nothing will change that. Give Mike the coat. It will be okay."

Joshua took off the coat gave it to Mike and walked back to the car. A faint chorus of music flowed through Joshua. *I am His child forever... I am His child forever.*

A realization struck Thomas—that Joshua had truly become a favorite of heaven; that this meager life pleased Yeshua, and even now the glory of the Lord shown with ever increasing brilliance. Joshua didn't hear heaven's music, or see the light shining through him, for he could barely keep from pounding his own head. But Thomas saw it and became swept up in it, floating and moving with the music. This is what I want, thought Thomas. "... O Lord, have mercy."

Whoosh.

No Room for Pride

Thomas found himself in the gray mist, standing, looking up at Joshua. "What happened back there?" asked Thomas. "You almost succumbed to rage, but instead gave up your coat and walked away. Then I saw the heavens open and…"

"I began to reflect the glory of Yeshua," Joshua chimed in.

"How? You didn't do anything."

"That's all anyone can do—nothing but trust God. I believed that I was a child of God no matter what others thought, including myself. The power of faith in Yeshua is the power that makes us like Him."

"So just like that you became what you are now?"

"Oh no. God had to work courageously in me over my lifetime. After all, I had a lot to overcome, but God is faithful to finish what He has begun."

"This still doesn't make sense," said Thomas. "God gives you all of… His glory… His grandeur simply because you trust Him? What about all the people who have done so much good? Don't they deserve anything?"

"You mean don't you deserve something."

"Well, yes, I know there are others who have done more, and I fully expect they should get more. But, I know my life doesn't deserve to be tossed aside and left for the black hole. That should be reserved for the Hitlers of the world. I would think I am above average in goodness for all I achieved."

Joshua winced at Thomas' last statement. "Where would you have put me in your ranking?" he inquired.

"Ahhh…" Thomas hesitated.

"I doubt I am even on your scale. The truth is, I could do nothing right, because my brain didn't function in a way that let me remember right from wrong. I went through life repeating the same mistakes, never learning. Fetal Alcohol Syndrome made my life hopeless. But thank God, He made life about trusting in Yeshua. That I could do. He saved me for His glory, not my glory. That is why I reflect Him so well—it is all about Him and not about me. I am nothing without Jesus, yet, He has chosen to produce the fullness of Himself in me."

"You didn't answer my question," protested Thomas. "What about all those who have achieved good things? Does God cast aside all their effort? Does faith in God allow those who have done nothing to leap-frog over a long life of sacrifice and work for the good of mankind? If that's how it is, why bother doing anything?"

"For those given much, much is expected. For those given little, little is expected. But all are to make an offering of what they have been given to be used by God for His Kingdom." Joshua continued. "Everything done on your own effort without God may be good, but they're temporary and have no eternal purpose. Everything done by faith through His power fits into God's perfect plan. By doing it His way, He protects you from pride and allows you to reflect His glory in a dark world. Reflecting that light to others has consequences that far outweigh any human endeavor. I want you to see not only the way of faith, but also the why. Life is not about what you achieve by having faith in yourself, but what God does through you when you trust in Him. It is God who then directs every action and becomes the goal of every thought. By trusting Yeshua, life gains purpose through faith, not by works, so there is no room for pride."

"No room for pride?" sneered Thomas, "I know a few people who didn't have enough pride in their work. Instead of doing it right, they covered their sloppiness with God's will. I quickly learned not to trust people who slung around God's name all the time."

"O Thomas," implored Joshua, "Don't let someone's hypocrisy blind you to the need to believe in Yeshua and trust Him. Faith does not circumvent the responsibility to put forth your best effort but instead enhances it. I trusted that God could somehow use my messed up life and my broken brain for His glory. Faith allowed me to breathe and go forward despite my struggle with Fetal Alcohol Syndrome. Do you remember what it said about faith on the back of the jacket Yeshua gave me?"

"Justified by faith," said Thomas. After a pause he added, "That's just my point—it's too simple, and leaves room for someone to take advantage."

"Yeah,… simple, just what I needed. Any other way, and I would've been left out. As far as allowing hucksters to take advantage— don't worry, God sees the heart."

"But why am I left out? I didn't cut any corners, I gave medicine my best." implored Thomas.

"Because you demand your way instead of God's way of faith. Come, you have more to learn." Joshua reached out and placed his hand on Thomas, "Lord, open the eyes of his heart."

Whoosh.

I'm His Child

"When can I have my motorcycle jacket back?" Joshua badgered Mike.

"You have been asking that question daily for two weeks, and my answer is the same—when I am certain you didn't steal the coat," said Mike.

Thomas felt the anger build in Joshua with each rebuff, and soon a battle raged in him. "He'll never give it back," said an angry voice somewhere in Joshua. "Just take it and get away from this place. Mike doesn't care, he just wants the coat for himself."

During this, Thomas wondered, *I don't see any glory of heaven here…how is a life based on faith any better than my way?*

For days Joshua's turmoil churned. He even hit his head once but immediately pulled back, trying hard to hold on to one thought—"I am God's child forever."

After a few days, Mike came up to Joshua's bedroom with the coat. He knocked on the door, "Josh, open the door."

A voice came from the bedroom, "I'm not Josh anymore, I am Joshua now." Joshua cracked the door to peer out, but when he saw his coat, he swung the door open. "My motorcycle jacket!"

"You may have the coat back on the following conditions," said Mike. "You promise to give the coat to the owner, if he ever turns up to claim it, and you will behave—keep your temper in check, no hitting, kicking or biting." Joshua shook his head up and down and grabbed for the coat. "Wait Joshua, I want to check the coat to make sure of its condition before I give it to you." He turned it around and seemed surprised at how nice the coat appeared. Joshua fidgeted, eager to hold it again, but Mike held up his hand. "I need to check a few more things. You need to take good care of this jacket or I will take it away again."

Mike checked the seams for any tearing and lastly looked in the zippered pockets. There he found an envelope with "for Joshua" written on the front.

"My note from the stranger," Joshua yelled. "I forgot all about it."

"Well, it is addressed to you, but if you want I'll read it to you," Mike said, knowing Joshua could barely read.

Joshua's hands were shaking with excitement as he carefully unsealed the envelope and handed the contents to Mike.

"To Joshua, God's child—"

"See I told you," Joshua interrupted. He could barely contain himself.

Mike read on. "Always remember it pleases Yeshua when you trust Him, especially when you feel bad, and God will be faithful to keep you until we will meet again in heaven."

As Mike looked up, Joshua couldn't stop dancing from excitement, "Okay, settle down. This is a bit of a mystery. I know you couldn't have written this, so tell me who wrote this note?"

"The man who gave me the coat wrote it. Why don't you believe me!"

"Here take the jacket and the letter," said Mike, "but you need to act like a child of God if you're going to claim to be one."

"Yes, I will," Joshua shouted out. "I trust God now."

Mike left shaking his head, "I'll believe it when I see it."

Joshua quickly put on the jacket, folded the letter carefully and put it back in the zippered pocket. He spent the rest of the day walking around in his motorcycle jacket telling everyone what it said on the back. Every few minutes, he would unzip the pocket, and carefully take out the letter to look at it. Running his finger over the words Joshua would say, "I am God's child forever."

After a few hours of Joshua strutting around in his coat, one of the other house members, Robert, became irritated. "Shut up!" Robert said, putting his fingers in his ears. "I am sick of hearing 'I am God's child.' Enough already."

From his facial features, Thomas could see that Robert had Down Syndrome, with a button nose, glasses, short pear-shaped body and no neck. However, he spoke clearly and had the typi-

108

cal nasal voice. Robert appeared to be high func-
tioning, and because of his higher skill level, he
cast himself as leader over the other members of
the group home. Like Joshua, he needed to be
somebody.

"To me you are still stupid ol' Josh,"
Robert continued. "I don't care what your letter
says. Besides, I know you can't read. I think you
are making this all up, because you don't like me
thinking better than you."

Joshua's temper flared so fast Thomas felt
his head spin. One moment Josh appeared calm,
the next his anger erupted toward Robert, his
hands clenched ready to strike. *Make him hurt!*
pounded through Joshua's mind and into his
right arm.

Thud, Joshua hit Robert on the chest, but
without much force, for something inside made
Joshua pull his punch into a slight tap. Then in
another rush of anger, Joshua wanted to knock
the smile off Robert's face, but again something
held him back at the last second.

Inside Joshua, Thomas witnessed a battle
being waged. Thoughts and emotions kept crash-
ing about, each vying for attention and adding to

the chaos. Underlying all this turmoil Thomas noticed a familiar foul stench swirling about. The same odor that had pursued him in the gray mist. *That foul smell is trying to get Joshua! Could that evil be the same darkness that pursued me in the gray lands?* The thought of an evil being prowling about trying to steal souls always seemed childish to Thomas, like the boogeyman under your bed. But he couldn't deny this entity was at the bridge, the gray lands and now working hard to amp up Joshua's rage.

Joshua's mind continued to swirl with ugly thoughts as the voice of darkness peppered his mind with taunts of anger and shame. *Hit Robert in the mouth, that will teach him. He's just as dumb as you.* Thomas watched as Josh's anger morphed into hateful fury. *Show Robert what for... teach him a lesson about pain that he'll never forget.*

The sheer strength of ugliness badgering Joshua worried Thomas. *Joshua is out of control. No matter how much Joshua tries, his alcohol ad-dled brain is not going to hold back this rage. Where is Yeshua? How can faith help Joshua? His damaged mind lacks any rudiments to fight this. Why doesn't God step in and deal with this?* Joshua started to

hit himself. Thomas waited for Yeshua to intervene, but nothing happened. Joshua hit himself
again even harder. *Faith doesn't matter much here,*
thought Thomas. The weak child part of Joshua
accepted each blow as punishment he deserved,
and Yeshua did nothing.

God, where are You? Thomas screamed.
Don't you care? Can't you see?… do something!

"I am too God's child…" whispered
Joshua. Bam! another hit. "Yeshua said so."
Joshua'a arm went limp.

Robert yelled, "Josh hit me, Josh hit me,
and he's hitting himself again." Stirring the whole
house into an uproar.

Mike came racing in from the kitchen,
"What's going on."

"Josh hit me after I asked him to be quiet,"
Robert said with a fake whine of being hurt. "He
thinks he is big stuff with that motorcycle jacket."

"My name is not Josh, it's Joshua. And I
am God's child… forever, and you can't do anything about it."

"Josh did you hit Robert?" asked Mike.

"Yes, but not as hard as I should've,"
Joshua said still wrestling with his anger.

"Go up to your room," Mike said. "I will be up in a few minutes." Joshua turned and ran up the stairs, trying to hide all the tears that tumbled out. A few minutes later Mike knocked on the door... "Joshua, open up so we can talk."

Joshua opened the door to let Mike in. "Give me the coat; I warned you about hitting. You have failed to abide by the rules of this house, and I can't keep overlooking it. So hand it over. I'll give it back when you have kept your temper under control for seven days in a row."

"Please don't take my jacket. I just can't help it when I get angry and upset." From inside Joshua, the emotions started to swirl again. *Reject... reject... you are nothing but a reject. You'll never get your jacket back. You're a failure; Yeshua doesn't want a failure. He saved you once, but he won't save you again, because like a dummy you've messed up again, even while wearing his jacket. That's a big no-no.*

Thomas, hearing this, knew it to be darkness talking and became angry over the torment being inflicted upon this defenseless boy. *God, Joshua has the mind of a child... are You just going to stand there? Why are You even letting evil speak*

like that to one who claims to be Your child? Isn't his
life tough enough with Fetal Alcohol Syndrome?
Where's the justice and love in all this?

"Josh," Mike stood firm, unaware of the
battle going on in Joshua. "The coat, please."

Joshua cried as he handed over the jacket.
"Can you read the back to me before you go… I
keep forgetting what it says."

Mike held the coat up and read, "Justified
by Faith… saved by Yeshua… God's child
forever." As Mike folded the jacket over his arm,
the envelope fell out of the unzipped pocket.
Mike picked it up to stuff it back in the coat, but
then turned and handed the letter to Joshua.

"You can keep it to remind you of the coat
and hopefully help you hold your temper," said
Mike.

Joshua took a deep breath, "Mike would
you read the letter to me. I need to hear the
words."

Mike removed the paper from the envelope, unfolded it, and began, "To Joshua a child
of God forever—always remember it pleases
Yeshua when you trust Him, especially when you

feel bad, and God will be faithful to keep you until we will meet again in heaven."

Joshua sighed and let his shoulders slump.

"Josh, maybe you're putting too much faith in these words. After all, they are just words on a piece of paper," consoled Mike.

The dark rumbling in Joshua's mind started up again, *How can God accept you when you hit Robert while wearing a jacket bearing his name? You are a disgrace to Yeshua. Besides, if God lets you off this time, you know you will just forget and do it again. How many chances do you get? You have a damaged brain; you will never be right in the head. Your life is a curse to yourself and to everyone around you. You're a piece of garbage and would be better off dead.*

The emotional barrage took a toll on Joshua, crippling his hope in the words on the jacket—hope of a life worth living.

Mike gazed at Joshua, waiting for some response.

"Maybe I have messed up too many times..." Joshua sighed. His mind swirled with ugly thoughts—*You're just trash littering up life. You even messed up killing yourself.*

He looked at the coat and the letter in Mike's hand. "Hey, there is more writing on the back. Read it to me."

Mike turned over the page and read aloud:

"Dear Joshua, part of being God's child is asking for mercy when you don't deserve it. A second part is trusting that God forgives you when you don't deserve it. The third part is seeking and receiving forgiveness over and over again for as long as you live. Remember, I love you, and I died to take away all your troubles and wrongs. This is why you are God's child forever. Forgiveness by faith in Yeshua will never run out. Signed Yeshua."

Mike handed the paper to Joshua without saying anything, turned around and left with the jacket.

A perplexed look came over Joshua. *I want to believe, but it's hard… If God will help my believing I think I could believe in spurts… What else is there for me, except to believe?… But then I'll mess up and get angry.*

Thomas saw the struggle in Joshua and became indignant. *Why doesn't God just heal Joshua's brain? Isn't that what faith is supposed to do? What good is faith if Joshua constantly has to fight the same battles with Fetal Alcohol Syndrome?*

Joshua struggled with his thoughts and prayed: *Lord, Have mercy on me 'cause my brain don't work right, I can't do it.*

"Yes, Lord, where is Your mercy?" whispered Thomas.

Whoosh.

Becoming What You Worship

The gray mist swirled around Thomas as he once again struggled to get his bearings. He desperately wanted to talk with Joshua about what had just happened before the grayness dimmed his recollection of what he had just experienced in Joshua's life. Looking around, Thomas saw Joshua standing with his arms raised, looking up. His face glowed in golden light pouring down upon him. His lips were moving, but Thomas couldn't quite hear, so he moved closer even

though the light made him uncomfortable.
Thomas heard Joshua softly singing:

"You turned my wailing into dancing;

you removed my sackcloth and clothed me
with joy,

that my heart may sing to you and not be
silent.

O Lord my God, I will give you thanks
forever."

Thomas grew impatient waiting for Joshua
to finish his song and finally interrupted. "Joshua,
I must know why."

"Why what?" Joshua said, lowering his
hands.

"Back in your former life negative thoughts
inundated you to the point you came close to being swept away. I want to know why God left you
to fight through such an onslaught of darkness
and doubt.

Joshua smiled, "You're right, my life was
very difficult and easily toppled into anger and all
sorts of ungodly things, but you're wrong about
God leaving me."

Thomas quickly went on with his own line
of thinking. "The war going on in you would

have been too much even for someone with normal intelligence. It makes no sense to me—God wants you to have faith, yet makes no effort to help when evil is dragging you under. Where's the good in that?"

Joshua looked at Thomas. "You think faith is about removing our hurts and pains, when in truth, faith is for keeping our eyes upon Jesus and letting Him sustain us through the trials of life." Then Joshua raised his arms again and sang:

"You reached down from on high and took hold of me;

You drew me out of deep waters.

You rescued me from my powerful enemy,

from my foes, who were too strong for me."

Thomas again interrupted Joshua, "There is another part of faith that bothers me. That note in the jacket's pocket telling you to ask for mercy and just trust that God forgives you. I have heard all this faith stuff before and have seen plenty of people treat it as some magical saying that wipes out any wrong they have done, then they go out and do the same things all over again. Isn't that an invitation to take advantage of God's forgiveness, by saying the magic words, but doing nothing to change? It's a license to do whatever you want, followed by a brief prayer for mercy… seems hypocritical and wrong to me."

Joshua looked over at Thomas in puzzlement, "First you fault God for making it too tough on me because of my disability—that He didn't do enough. Then you turn around and complain that He does too much, and I will resort to abusing the name of Jesus. God in His wisdom set it up for us to relate to Him through faith, because that way we remain under His protection, His strength, not our own. By humbly trusting in Jesus for all things, we are safe from all evil, including insincerity and pride. Sad is the person who refuses to trust Jesus because they feel they didn't do anything to deserve being a child of God. What is grace for if not for when we don't deserve it?"

Joshua turned to look at heaven's brightness and a song of praise broke out:

"You watched over me and made my way secure.

In Your faithfulness my faith did blossom till I became pleasing in Your sight."

When Joshua finished, he stood up and looked at Thomas. "Do you understand? It is all about God and nothing about me, even when it comes to faith. With faith even the most mentally disabled person can come to God with no understanding by just trusting in Jesus, and the greatest philosopher will need to put aside their intellect and trust as a child."

Joshua shone brightly of heaven's glory. The brilliance made Thomas insignificant and naked in the burning light.

After a slight pause Joshua spoke again, "As for taking advantage of God's grace—you are a fool if you think that God cannot read the heart of everyone who comes before Him. Whatever you put your faith in you will worship, and what you worship determines what you become. For my whole life I wanted to be free of the curse of Fetal Alcohol Syndrome. Trusting in Yeshua changed all that, transforming my curse into a blessing by which I became His child."

"Fetal Alcohol Syndrome will never be a blessing." objected Thomas.

"O Thomas, you are so blind. I am not calling Fetal Alcohol Syndrome the blessing. But, God used my disability to mold me and bring glory to His name. That's the blessing. Fetal Alcohol Syndrome took away any confidence in my own abilities and made me desperate for something more. It drove me to jump in despair from that bridge. When Yeshua saved me from dying in that river, He became my reason to live—my hope, my purpose, my life. In that moment, God changed my life from a curse to a blessing, and a day doesn't go by I don't thank Him for saving me. I would have settled for just being made normal, but God had much greater plans."

"You're saying faith can make any curse into a blessing?" questioned Thomas.

"Your entire life you placed your faith in yourself. You eventually became a much revered scientist and physician. On the other hand, I could do nothing worthy of such accolades. Jesus became my hope. I trusted Him to make in me something from nothing. Now, here at heaven's door all things become known, and we see the truth of each life—I reflect Yeshua, and you reflect yourself. So tell me, which path led to a blessing and which a curse?"

"That's not fair," protested Thomas. "I blessed many lives on earth, but obviously there is no need for the medical profession here."

"There you go again relying on what you can do, rather than upon God," Joshua said shaking his head. "The abyss is full of self-reliant souls who have spent their lives trusting in themselves instead of learning to trust God."

"So am I to be condemned for trusting in myself?" asked Thomas.

"Again you're relying on what you can do. Everyone in the black hole feels there has been some mistake, that they deserve far better than being left in the dark to fend for themselves. They blame God for granting them what they have worked their whole lives to get—their own way. Everyone in heaven knows they don't deserve to be there, and everyone in hell thinks they've been cheated and curse God for all their woes. The first group loves and worships God because they have been forgiven. In gratitude, they fall before the throne of grace, praising Yeshua for giving them what no amount of human effort could achieve—life in Jesus."

Jesus? thought Thomas. It annoyed him a little. *I mean really, it's okay for kids and the simple-minded, but really for a doctor...*

"I see your mind is stumbling over the cornerstone of life," Joshua said as he gazed at Thomas. "I think you need to see another bit of my life to help you understand."

Joshua reached out and put his hand on Thomas.

Whoosh.

Joshua stood before a closed door at the group home. The nameplate on the door read "Robert." Below it a hand written sign had been taped up, "KEEP OUT." Joshua banged on the door with his head trying to control his temper. "Open the door, Robert."

"You can't come in unless I say so," said Robert. "This is my room and my stuff. Go away, or I'll yell for Mike."

"I don't want any of your stupid stuff," said Joshua, "and I won't go away until you say you're sorry for what you blabbed at dinner tonight."

"Why should I be sorry? Can't you handle the truth?" remarked Robert. "Everyone knows you wet your bed last night. Michael should put you back in diapers."

"You don't know nothing. I had a seizure."

"You always blame things on your seizures, but I think you're just a big baby."

"Come here, I'll show you who's a baby," Joshua said as he clenched his fist and rattled the doorknob.

"You better not touch me, or you'll get kicked out of here."

"I'll kick you out of here." Joshua felt his temper starting to take over. "Now open up. I won't hit; I just want to talk."

Robert opened the door and quickly sat on his bed. He held a framed family photo to his chest for protection. It showed him standing between his parents wearing a medal he had won at Special Olympics.

Joshua stood in the doorway and spoke with a slight crack in his voice, "You're a mean person and need to say you're sorry."

"Oh, yeah… At least I have parents who love me. Your parents left you, so if you get kicked out of here, you'll be living in a dumpster… garbage boy," Robert said in a sing-song way meant to ridicule Joshua.

Joshua's temper surged. His jaw clenched, and he stepped into the room to pound Robert.

"Mike! Josh wants to hurt me," Robert said slipping past Joshua and running down the hall.

Joshua returned to his room and slammed the door. Tears welled up in his eyes as he looked around the room—lava lamp, posters of baseball players and motorcycles, but no pictures of family.

Knock, knock. "Joshua, this is Michael, open the door so we can talk."

"Open it yourself," Joshua said, trying to hide his hurt.

Michael opened the door to see Joshua sprawled on his bed facing the wall.

"Okay, tell me what happened between Robert and you."

"I want to find my mother and father," said Joshua. "I need to know."

"How does that have anything to do with...Did Robert say something about your parents?" asked Mike. Joshua could only nod his head. Mike went on, "I am not so sure that is a good idea, because it may cause you more hurt than you already have."

"You know where you come from, and Robert has pictures of him and his parents. I have nothing... I know nothing... I remember nothing... I am nothing."

"All right," said Mike, "you can give it a try, but you'll have to do this on your own. I will put you in touch with the Child Protective Services social worker. They may have a way to track down your parents... Tell me, what are you going to do if you find them?"

"I need to ask them why."

"Why covers a lot of area, is there a specific question you have?" asked Mike.

"Yes," said Joshua looking hard at Mike. "I want to know why they made me like this."

"You mean why your mom drank during the pregnancy and then left?"

"Yeah." said Joshua, rubbing his eyes to hide his tears.

"You may be disappointed," responded Mike, then under his breath added, "if you get any answer at all."

Joshua turned back to face the wall, "I don't care. I need to ask."

"Okay, I'll call this afternoon and arrange an appointment for you," said Mike as he closed the door.

WHY… WHY… WHY? raced through Joshua's mind. *She didn't love me enough to stop drinking and raise me! I want to hear her tell me why.* For the next two days Thomas heard Joshua repeat these same thoughts over and over in an endless stream of hurt.

This is crazy, thought Thomas. *She's an alcoholic. If she is still alive, what can she say to make things any different?*

But Joshua's thoughts kept repeating, stuck on *why, Why, WHY*. Soon, it became hard to think of anything else. Finally, Thomas couldn't take it anymore, "This is pointless; I am learning nothing. Why do I need to experience this? Lord have mercy." Thomas waited expecting to be whisked back to the gray mist, but nothing happened. "Lord have mercy!" he tried again, but still nothing. Slowly Thomas began to feel angry toward God for all the unanswered questions... the pointless hurts... the silence.

Ten days later.

"Ms. Gabriel from Child Protective Services is here to talk to you," Mike said rousing Joshua from his despondency. Joshua walked down the stairs to the living room, apprehensive about what she would tell him.

She sat on the sofa with a file open in front of her, dressed in a dark blue pants suit looking very businesslike. She looked up at Joshua with her dark brown eyes and a soft brown face. She smiled and beckoned with her hand for Joshua to sit next to her on the sofa.

"I understand you want to meet your birth mother," said Ms. Gabriel. "But before I tell you about her, let me ask you a few questions." Joshua sat down quite taken by her warm soft voice and nodded his head. "I have been told you tried to kill yourself a few months ago but were saved by a stranger who gave you his motorcycle jacket."

"Yes," said Joshua, watching her lips and eyes speak more than her words.

"That he gave you the name Joshua along with his jacket."

"Yes," said Joshua as he began letting go of some of his sadness.

"Do you know what Joshua means?"

"Not really." Joshua felt a thrill run through him when she said his name.

"It means 'Jehovah saves,' and Jehovah is the Hebrew name for God. Now if God saved you and gave you his name, what does that say about you?"

"That I am His child." Joshua said with slight hesitation.

"I want you to say it again, but this time like you are standing before the throne, and all heaven is listening waiting to cheer at the miracle God has done."

Joshua took a deep breath and exhaled. "I am God's child."

"Can you hear them shouting praise for all that God has done in you?"

"I... I think so... maybe."

"Do you know what makes this even more amazing—what elevates the rejoicing of heaven to even higher levels?" asked Ms. Gabriel.

Joshua pondered, but then gave up and shrugged his shoulders.

"It is the triumph of Jesus over your troubled life. What hell intended for your destruction God used for His glory. He transformed you from an abandoned child with Fetal Alcohol Syndrome to a glorious child of God Almighty, the Creator of the Universe. Now, that is something to cheer about." Ms. Gabriel said. Her smile lit up the room.

"But I don't feel cheery," said Joshua, "and I still got a temper."

"It is not about cheerful feelings, Joshua. The jubilation of heaven is about what God has done. God made you His child by His word. That way all of it depends on Him and His faithfulness. You can't bungle this. You just need to believe Him. For your temper you get a helper, the Holy Spirit."

Joshua, for the first time in days, began to relax. The suffocating feelings of rejection that had been bubbling and churning in him drifted away.

"Now, about your birth mother," Ms. Gabriel said opening the file. "Her first name is Tammy. She requested no other personal information be given out. When she was arrested for child abuse, you were removed from her care by the state. She went through court mandated drug and alcohol treatment but relapsed before the end of her probationary period. No one is sure where she is now, or if she is even alive."

"Did… did she ever want me?" Joshua asked.

"I don't know; she was not given the choice." Ms. Gabriel placed her hand on top of Joshua's and went on, "Based on her continuing problems, the court decided that it would be safer for you not to return to her care. A pediatric medical examiner, Dr. Thomas Jones, documented significant problems with Fetal Alcohol Syndrome and severe Reactive Attachment Disorder. He recommended no further contact with the mother."

"I remember biting him. I didn't like him, now I know why—he took me from my mother. Bad, bad,… bad man."

Living through this moment feeling Joshua's pain, Thomas gasped. *I only wanted what would be best for this boy. He took it all wrong! His mother couldn't take care of herself, let alone a child with severe disabilities. It's her fault, she did this, not me! It's not fair, I was just doing my job. If I am being condemned for this, I demand a chance to defend myself.*

"Joshua, your mother agreed with that ruling. That's why she asked that her last name be withheld and agreed not to contact you. She knew her drinking caused your disability, and I am sure her sorrow is great. I can't imagine the burden she carries knowing her actions damaged you."

"And my father?"

"He never came forward, and your mother never identified him. It is likely that he doesn't even know he has a son," said Ms. Gabriel, gazing intently at Joshua. "I know this all must hurt terribly. I am sorry."

Joshua looked down trying to cover his tears and shame. He just wanted… to die.

"Joshua," Ms. Gabriel's voice penetrated his heartache. "The thoughts you have will drag you down into dark places. This is not what Yeshua intended when He saved you and made you His child."

"What does He want in me? My mother and father are bad… I am bad… I'm broken and no good."

"As a child of God and part of His family, you have been given a most powerful gift," said Ms. Gabriel.

"What gift is that?" Joshua questioned.

"Forgiveness of course, God's gift to you through which you have become His child. What's more, it's a gift to be given to others, so that through forgiveness you become like Yeshua. You can even give it to your parents."

"How do I forgive someone when they are not here, and I don't even know who they are or if they're alive?"

"It's a gift unhampered by anything of this world. It all depends on you forgiving like Jesus forgives you. When you forgive, it testifies of your own forgiveness."

"Well, I still don't understand, but if it will please Yeshua, then I will do it for Him." Joshua bowed his head. "I forgive my mother, and I forgive my father."

"I think there are still others you need to forgive," said Ms. Gabriel.

"Okay, I forgive Dr. Jones, and I even forgive Robert." Looking up at Ms. Gabriel, Joshua asked, "Is there anyone else?"

"Yes, you need to forgive yourself."

"That's a hard one, because I know all the bad things I have done."

"Has God forgiven you?"

"I think so, but sometimes I don't feel like it."

"Remember, it is a faith thing, not a feeling thing."

"Okay, I guess I'll forgive myself too."

"I am proud of you Joshua," said Ms. Gabriel as she closed Joshua's file.

"Ms. Gabriel, would you do something for me? If you run into my mother, or my father...

or even Dr. Jones, tell them I forgive them, and I would like to tell them myself."

"Yes, I will."

"Oh, one other thing, tell them my brain may be hard to live with and not work right, but my heart trusts in Yeshua, who saved me, gave me a new name and made me His child. I hope their lives find the same blessing in Jesus."

Thomas was stunned. *What did I do that needs forgiveness? I was just doing my job. Maybe I should have been less abrupt and a little more caring, but I had a full schedule that got messed up from that bite. I'm the one who should be forgiving Joshua!* Humph, forgiveness is just a bunch of religious rubbish used to cover up errors. But hearing Joshua forgive his parents and then to address it to him, broke a dam that held a lifetime of slights and mistakes and lack of being merciful. Thomas saw with clarity how much he had missed by not forgiving nor asking to be forgiven. Sadly he thought: *It's too late, I can't go back in time to set right what I've spent a lifetime ignoring.* "Lord have mercy." he whispered wondering if mercy would ever be enough.

Whoosh.

Thomas found himself back in the gray
mist with Joshua standing nearby. He felt shame
for having treated Joshua as a damaged human,
rather than a person filled with worth and meaning. How could he have been so calloused? A
strong desire arose to tell Joshua how sorry he felt
and ask for forgiveness. *No, it's too late, it would
never match the hurt and appear hypocritical.* He
then thought of his plan to give flowers to his
daughter hoping it would make up for his years
of failing as her father. *What kind of Father have I
been for her?* He shuddered thinking he had been
just like his father... *No I don't deserve forgiveness.*

As Thomas struggled with his feelings,
Joshua spoke, "Thomas, I forgive you, the Lord
has granted my prayer to allow me to tell you in
person. He has given me the added privilege of
telling you of His infinite forgiveness and mercy. I
hope my life story has blessed you, for Yeshua
truly made life a blessing to me. Now it is time
for me to leave you and return to my place at the
feet of Yeshua. Goodbye, and remember the
Lord's mercy is new every morning. The name

'Jesus' will never lose its power to forgive and transform. You just need to put your faith in Him to become His child forever." Joshua's face shown at the glory before him, he walked into the light, then in a blinding flash—disappeared. When Thomas's eyes recovered, everything had returned to gray, and he found himself alone in the mist.

"Hello… what do I do now?" called out Thomas. "Joshua, are you there? I accept your apology…"

Silence.

Thomas couldn't tell how long he stood there waiting for a response. Finally he decided, "I'll just follow Joshua." After a few tentative steps, it became obvious that he had no idea as to which direction to go. Then he thought of Joshua's warning about falling into the pit and stopped. That's when the scent of decay and the sound of gurgling caught his attention. Thomas froze in fear. He turned slowly, trying to deter-mine the source of the foul odor and sound, but again the mist hid everything beyond a few feet away.

Gurgle slurp

It's stalking me! Thomas tried to control his panic, and fought the urge to gag with each breath. He could taste the rot and knew it was out there. Would this be how life would end? In an act of desperation he called out, "Lord, have mercy!"

Chapter 4 - Elena

Hope is the lamp that leads us out of darkness into light.

"To them God has chosen to make known among the Gentiles the glorious riches of this mystery, which is Christ in you, the hope of glory." Col.1:27

"For God, who said, "Let light shine out of darkness," made his light shine in our hearts to give us the light of the knowledge of the glory of God in the face of Christ." 2 Corinthians 4:6

The Dancing Princess

As Thomas waited and waited, a gnawing fear grew at the edges of his mind that no one would come to his rescue. "I believe—" he called out, hoping it would bring Joshua back. "I want to believe… Please, Joshua, come back and help me," but nothing happened. Straining to listen,

Thomas only heard the slurping of oozing mud. He knew that sound, and with it came dread that shut down every thought—the fear of what waited in the dark.

"LORD, HAVE MERCY!" he shouted, hoping those words would provide a magical escape from what waited out there in the shroud of gray mist.

In the distance, Thomas thought he saw a faint glow. "Joshua! Come help me… the black hole, it's coming for me." The grayness shifted, and the glow faded to gray. Another moment and the fog closed in even thicker than before.

Slurp.

He rubbed his eyes, trying to clear the veil of fog. Nothing changed except his own growing apprehension. "Hello, Joshua, is that you?" Thomas called out. Fear made his voice break. "Please, Joshua, I need your help. This is no time to play games. Tell me it's you."

"Oh, I don't think he is coming back," came a strange female voice. "That kind prefers the burning light instead of being friends here with us."

Startled, Thomas called out, "Who's there? Are you stuck here like me?" This unfamiliar voice seemed friendly. In fact, it reminded Thomas of a voice he had heard on a trip to New Orleans. Walking down Bourbon Street, an attractive woman stood outside a strip club, and tried to seduce men to enter. He never succumbed, but he never forgot how alluring and soft her voice sounded. Beads of sweat ran down his forehead.

"I would sure like a friend. It can get pretty lonely in these gray lands," said the women. "Just keep walking toward my voice, and we'll get together."

Well, at least I have someone like myself for company, Thomas thought. *But how can I be sure?* An awkward silence followed, ramping up the apprehension of who stood just beyond his sight. "I want to go to the light, but it burns too hot for me to get close," Thomas blurted out, trying not to show his fear. "Maybe we could go together standing far enough away that it wouldn't hurt, but still give us light and keep the black hole away."

"Who needs that light? We can help each other find our way," said the voice "Come join me. We'll be a team.

Thomas hesitated, "No, I want the light, like I had with Joshua."

"Of course you do, but he's gone and won't be coming back. It's all a ruse to get you to come to that awful light until it burns you up," said the voice filled with concern.

"Who are you?... Are you here to help me?" Thomas asked, not sure of what approached him. "Please, I need to know I'll be safe with you."

"We can look out for each other," said the voice. "Let's explore this place together. If that light comes again, we can help each other get away from the burning."

"But, how do I know you are telling the truth? Show yourself—I want to see you. I just need assurance of your intentions."

"You can trust me. Why, I'll be whatever you want," the voice replied from somewhere to the left.

As Thomas turned, a putrid smell hit his nose. He shook himself, trying to keep from retching. "You're from that foul abyss."

"Oh Thomas, you're such a tease. You know we'll eventually be together. In fact, we already chose each other. Why fight it? There is no hope for you in that harsh light. Come, be with me and live in the luxurious darkness, where all your dreams become yours to possess, and all the pleasures of the world carry no shame, for nothing is exposed to that nasty light." The stink continued to close in, slowly encircling Thomas and tightening around his chest.

"I can't breathe. You're getting too close... I can't breathe!" Thomas cried, as the stench constricted about his throat. Again he called out to Joshua, "Lord have mercy!... Yeshua."

"Don't you think it's a little late for the religious words? Not that they hold any power, but I think you sound a little ridiculous saying that name. Face it, there is no help coming; it's all a fairytale. Look at yourself, a big shot doctor crying out like a helpless baby."

"I..." Thomas wheezed, "I can't catch my breath."

"Let yourself go. It will be over quickly. Just relax and slip into my realm. We can be together forever."

Thomas closed his eyes, trying to inhale. The strain left him about to black out when a faint song filled the air with music. As it continued to grow, the darkness began to lose its grip. Thomas breathed in the sweet notes. With each exhale, the foul odor drifted away. Finally, he took a deep breath of heaven's pure fragrance that tingled his lungs with joy. It reminded him of something he had lost long ago in his childhood—the refreshing air of purity and innocence. A glowing figure pushed the awful smell away and replaced it with the fragrance of wild flowers in a pine forest. Thomas closed his eyes to take in its refreshing sweetness.

"Hi, I am Elena. The Lord heard your cry and sent me to sing for you."

Thomas opened his eyes, and beauty flooded his vision. As much as Joshua had the magnificence of heaven, Elena sparkled with heaven's unimagined beauty. Then Elena reached out and gave Thomas a hug that made him forget the fearful blackness and calmed his angst. "Oh my,"

Thomas sighed. A soft peace bathed him like the morning sunshine after a night of rain. He wanted to breathe it all in and never let it out, to stay in this moment forever.

"Out goes the bad air, in comes the good," Elena released Thomas and laughed with joy. The melody coming from her lips made Thomas tingle with life. Though he did not understand how, Elena's loveliness commanded all thoughts to rise up and join in the joyous song of life. Thomas could not take his eyes off of her. "O Thomas, do not be so enamored with what you see in me," she smiled. "I only reflect the beauty of my Redeemer who makes all things pure and beautiful." The music of her voice wrapped around Thomas, floating in and out like a gentle breeze. He had never felt such goodness before.

"Thomas, do you remember me?" Elena said, breaking into his thoughts.

"Ahh… no, I don't recall ever having met someone so beautiful as you."

"That is in part why I have been sent to help you. You've been ignoring beauty for your entire life, but the Lord still has hope for you."

"Ignore? How could I ignore someone as beautiful as you? You're…" Thomas searched for words to do justice for the vision before him.

"Careful Thomas," she said. "You need to worship the Creator and not His creation. My beauty is but a reason to bow before Him, who is the source of all beauty. Come and glorify God with me. Together we can give Him thanks for what you see in me."

Thomas gazed at Elena, trying to take it all in, but found the effort only distracted from the joy of the moment.

She laughed and joy burst forth like a fountain. She twirled and danced with boundless energy. He wished to join in but realized his movement lacked grace and only subtracted from the beauty.

Elena twirled and began again to sing:

"O Lord, our Lord, how majestic is your name in all the earth! You have set your glory above the heavens. From the lips of children and infants, you have ordained praise to silence Your enemies. You bring forth beauty in us to shame our ancient foe."

The notes of Elena's song stirred something deep in Thomas—flavors of life long forgotten and buried under piles of medical journals and treatment protocols.

She continued to dance and sing, "When I consider your heavens, the work of your fingers, the moon and the stars, which you have set in place, what am I that you are mindful of me, yet to me you have given grace and beauty, that I might sing of Thy glory."

Thomas couldn't stop himself from trying to join in the dancing. Soon, Thomas became exhausted and had to put his hands on his knees to catch his breath. He looked at Elena and gasped, "I can't keep up."

Elena kindly stopped, and they both sat down to enjoy the blessing of the moment. Thomas noticed that he felt somehow important to her, not from anything he had done, but for just being there—truly refreshing.

Staring at Thomas, Elena said, "How good it is to meet you again. I can't help but give God praise for all He did through our meeting on earth, AND has done in my life since. Grace upon grace He has showered upon me, filling me to overflowing with praise of Him who is the essence of life."

Thomas barely heard her as his mind continued to soak in the joy that poured forth from her. Finally he had to ask, "How can I learn to sing and dance like you?" His question startled him as he spoke. *Has her beauty made me a stupid fool? I don't even like to sing and dance.*

"Praising God for all He is doing happens when you stop running after lesser things. Dancing before God is not stupid or foolish. Worship and praise to God helps clear your eyes for seeing and open your ears to hear."

"I am sorry; I didn't mean to be disrespectful. I forgot you people can read minds. The truth is, what I see and hear now is beyond anything I've ever imagined," apologized Thomas.

"Thomas, this small joy you have seen blossoming in me is nothing compared to beholding the beauty of the Lord, and my song is but the first note of heaven's musical score."

"How can anything be more pleasing than what I see and hear in you?" said Thomas.

"Believe me, His glory is far greater than anything you can imagine," Elena said with an explosion of joyful laughter. Then she sang:

"Ascribe to the Lord the glory due his name;

Worship the Lord in the splendor of his holiness."

When she had finished Thomas became curious, "How can you say we have met before? I know I would have remembered someone as beautiful as you."

"You compare me now to what you have seen in a world clouded by ungodliness. On earth, lust corrupts loveliness, pleasure is mistaken for joy, and they call everything good until goodness loses all meaning. What you see in me is a reflection of heaven—where everything mirrors God's glory and goodness. Yes, we have met before, but I'm afraid the things of earth have blinded you."

This stunned Thomas. "No, I don't think I would have overlooked you. Even in a crowd you would command everyone's attention. Besides, I've been a doctor most of my life and have trained myself to observe and judge people."

"Could it be you have been looking at the wrong things your whole life? In the light of heaven, the things of earth fade and are forgotten. For when you see God's everlasting goodness, there is nothing in all creation that compares to Him."

Thomas continued trying to remember where they had met before, but when she sang he no longer cared.

"My heart exults in the Lord;
For He has been mindful of my humble state
And exalted His name through me,
My mouth speaks boldly against the darkness,
Because I rejoice in Your salvation.
"There is no one holy like the Lord,
Indeed, there is no one besides You,
Nor is there any rock like our God.
Nothing can compare to You."

The song made Thomas want to get up and shout and move to God's glory, for each note touched him like nothing he had ever experienced before. That's when he again caught sight of his arms—gray, sickly skin smudged with dark blotches. A wave of shame washed over Thomas as he realized the truth of his appearance. *I am ugly and dirty, and Elena so beautiful. I am disgusting next to her.*

Elena saw a shadow come over Thomas and knew what troubled him. Gently she spoke, "Before His throne we gaze upon His infinite glory, and it causes us to sing praises unto our King. In heaven, nothing interferes with our worship. But if you were to come without being washed for the occasion and not properly dressed, you could not focus your attention on Him. You would be too self-consciousness of your own shame like you are now."

Thomas tried to hide his sores, but the more he tried the greater his self-loathing. "Oh Thomas, you're the only one looking at your shame. My attention is focused on my Lord Jesus."

"I am not looking at myself," Thomas objected, trying to hide his unsightly appearance.

"Let me make it a little easier to understand," Elena offered. "What if the Lord invited you to an elegant dinner at the King's palace. When you arrived, you discovered a big hole in the seat of your pants. You wouldn't be thinking about honoring the King, or how delicious the food tasted, or enjoying conversation with the other guests, because your mind would be concerned with the hole and trying to keep it hidden."

"So how do I... aah... get washed up and dressed for the banquet?" Thomas asked, still grappling with his feelings of humiliation.

"Let Jesus adorn you with His innocence and purity," she said.

"And how does that happen?"

Elena smiled, happy to be sharing such joyous news, "You must come to Him and be born again." Thomas winced at that old cliché, for it conjured up thoughts of squinty faced people waving their Bibles around. "I see that my words are insufficient to open your eyes," Elena said as she moved on.

"Don't give up on me," Thomas pleaded, not knowing what else to say but fearing she would leave.

"I think what you need is to experience genuine hope of glory, not the shallow wimpy hope of winning your medical accolades, or having a building named after you, but the actual hope of heaven."

It surprised Thomas that she knew of his life as a doctor back on earth. *Though Elena did say they had met before. Maybe she had rotated through his lab as a medical intern.* He decided not to object to her belittling all he had accomplished, for she seemed quite passionate about the hope of heaven, so he played along. "Tell me about this hope."

"I will do more than tell you, for just like Joshua did with you, I will show you from my life."

This I want to see, thought Thomas. *At least I'll figure out where we met before.* He found it quite enthralling to see himself through the eyes of others.

"Wanting to 'see' is a start," said Elena, reading Thomas' thoughts. "You only can see as great as your hope, and up to now you have placed your hope in meaningless things. That is why you are dressed in rags."

Thomas felt chagrin when he realized she knew what he had been thinking. After a long pause, he finally said, "I guess I have a lot to learn."

"The true hope of heaven is a gift from God for anyone who will truly let go of hoping in lesser things. For where your treasure is, there will be your heart."

"Hope of heaven? I always tried to give a more pragmatic hope to my patients based on medical science. Are you saying I was wrong?"

"The hope of earth is like a bandage, covering, but not healing the hurt. The hope of heaven leads to restoration of purity, beauty and innocence of the inmost being. Hoping for less is not true hope at all."

"You mean hoping to become like you?"

"No, Thomas," Elena cut in. "Like my redeemer... can't you see I am nothing without Jesus, but have everything with Him." Elena could tell Thomas did not fathom the hope of heaven, so she silently prayed—*Lord open his eyes to what he cannot see.* "We will go back to when I was truly nothing on earth, and where we first met. Perhaps there you will perceive what you have missed."

"Yes, please, I am curious what distracted me to keep me from noticing you."

"It will be similar to when Joshua took you into his life. What transpires you will comprehend even when it is an unfamiliar language. Even my own chaotic thoughts as a child will be open for you to see. For in the light of heaven nothing can be hidden, and you will understand and witness what transpires beyond earthly understanding."

Earthly understanding? Thomas pondered. *What does that mean? Could she be talking of some kind of miraculous healing? I don't recall witnessing any miracles in my career, at least none beyond the pale of medical science.* "Okay, I'm ready," said Thomas, eager for the adventure to begin.

Elena looked at Thomas and shook her head. "If the raw emotion and struggles in my life get to be more than you can handle, you can call out to the Good Shepherd, by saying 'my sweet Jesus,' and you will be pulled back here."

Thomas laughed to himself. *"'My sweet Jesus'... give me a break. I think I've seen the raw side of life before."*

"Thomas! Your pride is showing," said Elena. "Nothing goes unnoticed; even your thoughts and motives are exposed in His light. These words aren't to be used flippantly. They are a prayer to focus your attention on the truth of who is Lord over all. I suggest you treat His name as holy and do not regard it as too childish for your lips. You will see there is power and authority in His name."

Thomas felt indignation at being called out over some silly words which most people use as an exclamation. *Is this really that big a deal?*

"The words I have given you can provide you light—pointing to the glory of God and true life," admonished Elena. "But, I warn you misusing the same words can lead to hiding the truth and entrapment in death. All words come from the heart, and depending on how they are used, will affect the heart for good or evil. Come, I want to show you the power of these words in my life. But I need to caution you—the darkness in my life will shock you."

"Oh please, I'm a doctor, there isn't much I have not seen. Besides, if you survived to become such glory, I think I can…"

"Thomas, just as appalling as your lack of reverence for 'my sweet Jesus,' is your naiveté concerning the horror of darkness. It can snap you like a twig. I pray my life will give you a deeper understanding of both." Elena reached out and touched Thomas.

Thomas sank back excited and hoping to understand the mystery behind Elena.

Whoosh.

Less Than Nothing

Immediately Thomas fell into a thick oppressive gloom, a muddy darkness that seeped into his soul, producing dreadful thoughts that smothered any goodness in life. Every part of Elena's body felt locked in pain. Even breathing took effort to inhale the murky air against the pain of chest movement. *Where on earth could this be?* The abrupt plunge into Elena's life shocked Thomas by the weight of misery. He forced himself to think—*you can do this. No, you can do this* —repeating it over and over to keep focused. He had to stay in control and avoid slipping into a wild panic. Marshaling his determination, he refused to bow and say the words that would bail him out and send him back to the gray lands. How could he face Elena if after ten seconds of her life he wanted to run? He didn't want to appear like a fool for not... *Wait a minute, maybe that phrase, that phrase she gave me is meant to humiliate me!* Thomas jumped on the thought. *I probably did something to her that she didn't like, and now she is seeking to embarrass me by making me have to to say those words.* Then in the darkness it suddenly hit Thomas that in this horrid place he had forgotten the exact words to say. *Something Jesus.* Unfortunately, the only things that came to mind were swear words. "Eeeeehhh," Elena cried out, pulling Thomas back from this unbearable situation. *First, I must figure out where Elena has sent me. But how? I can't even think straight in this place.*

A noxious plug of mucus stuck in Elena's throat, making her gag and have the dry heaves which only caused more pain. Eeecckkk. Coughing finally cleared the mucus. *You're lost... you're worthless... you'd be better off dead,* pounded through Elena over and over, and each one pierced Thomas too.

I'm not sure I can survive this! Thomas' thoughts swirled like wraiths in the dark. The air thick with filth continued to choke any lucid thought. *I must be in the black hole! I've been tricked! What are the words to get out?*

Elena coughed and attempted to swallow, but her mouth adhered to where she lay with thick drool gluing her dry tongue to the roof of her mouth.

Control yourself, don't panic… you can figure a way out of this. Hang on. Unlike his experience in Joshua's life, he now felt utterly lost in the foreboding darkness that surrounded Elena.

"Unnnnh," pierced the darkness followed by "Ahiiieeeee."

Thomas could not only hear her screeching, but he also experienced the pain of her soul —alone in the dark. Each time she took another breath, another howl escaped her cracked lips. The sound of hopelessness—crying out from being abandoned, dead and forgotten. Thomas had never felt heaviness like this before. *If I had only this for my life, it would be better off to have never been born.* The horror of this evil place far outstripped anything Thomas had ever imagined.

How could this be Elena's life. The contrast from her beauty to this; something is wrong.

"Ahiiieeee, oowww," escaped from Elena's cracked lips as she strained to move.

How long does this go on? Is there no end to this agony? His mind began to erode with the feeling that each scream coming from Elena also came from his own soul. *Say the words, bailout before you go insane.* "Jesus... Elena... Jesus!"

Nothing.

His thoughts spun with alarm. He endeavored to divert his mind from the nagging fear and panic by trying to figure out where Elena had taken him. He noted under her body krinkled a stiff plastic sheet. The air dank with dust and the foul smell of urine and feces. Elena lay naked with only a grimy diaper that ripped at her raw bottom with any attempt to roll into a new position. The cold made Thomas shudder. When Elena tried to ease the pain in her joints, her skin stuck to the plastic sheet causing a feeling of tearing as the flesh ripped free. The torture of wanting to move yet severe pain with the effort made Elena and Thomas cry out.

"Ahiiieeeeee."

Lift your head so I can see what's going on.
Thomas sought to get Elena to move so he could
better orient himself to the situation. But Elena
only laid there in a pool of spittle, wailing like an
animal caught in a trap. Looking around, Thomas
noted there were metal bars barely visible in the
darkness. He finally surmised that it must be a
crib because above him hung a mobile with
cutout figures of farm animals. The only light for
the room came from a dingy window near the
ceiling. Boxes and cleaning supplies lined one
side of the small room, and at the far end a win-
dowless door. Muffled sounds came from the other side of the doorway along with a sliver of light
peeping from under the sill.

"Ahhiiieee," Elena cried, trying to get the
attention of someone from beyond the door. *Help
me... help me...* Elena's soul cried out with each
wailing breath.

*Does no one care that this poor girl is dying
in here?* Thomas couldn't believe that people
could walk past the door and ignore the plight of
Elena in this wretched supply closet.

"Ahhiiieee," she exhaled a painful howl,
trying to attract attention from those outside.

Nothing… followed by a squeal of pain as
Thomas tried to push and get her to move. Everything in Elena's existence seemed to be a prison,
keeping her trapped with no escape: the walls and
closed door of her dingy closet, the bars on the
crib, the plastic sheet sticking to her skin. Then
Thomas noticed one more horror of this dungeon. Around Elena's wrist a piece of duct tape
held her right hand to the bars of the crib. The
skin under the tape felt chafed and raw, making
any attempt to pull free painfully impossible. As a
result her fingers on that hand had curled from
disuse into a misshapen claw.

Where are we? Thomas searched for clues.
Who would keep a child in such deprivation? Suddenly he heard and felt a gurgling that made him
seize with fear. His mind envisioned the black
hole coming for them from the shadows. *I can't
take this anymore… whatever is going to happen get
it over with!* "Jesus help, Jesus… JESUS!"

Nothing.

Soon Thomas felt another gurgle along
with abdominal cramping in Elena. Phhhrrrrt.
Elena's diaper filled with stink and the malodor-
ous stool oozed down Elena's legs burning her

skin as it went. Laying in a mass of filth, Elena increased her wailing. Each cry ignited even more angst in Thomas. "Whaaaaaa." Thomas again had to fight to control his panic. *I can't live like this. I can't even breathe…* A scream of terror welled up in Thomas, and he sent it out into the darkness with Elena's cry. "Ahiiieeeeee!"

Suddenly, the sound of the doorknob turning sliced through the darkness. Both Elena and Thomas became quiet with anticipation. The door opened to a blinding light. A puff of fresh air blew in accompanied by a woman dressed in a white smock, her face hidden behind a surgical mask. She flipped on a light. Not a soft comforting light, but harsh blue glare from a bare fluorescent bulb that hung overhead. It flickered with an irritating irregularity, showing the bleak surroundings of a housekeeping supply closet.

"Akkkkkkk," Elena resumed her screaming.

"Elena, stop your screeching." The voice came from behind the mask. "No one likes it, that's why you're in here." She dropped the side of the crib and freed Elena's wrist from the duct tape by slipping it over her contorted hand.

"I don't have time to deal with your crying or the mess you make of your diaper. You're only supposed to get one change per day, you know."

Above Elena loomed a middle aged nurse, her brown hair tied back in a bun held in place with a red kerchief tied below her hair in back. She looked stern and spoke like someone upset over having more work to do than time to do it. "Waaaaa," Elena shrieked as the woman grabbed her legs, whipping her around to change the diaper. Thomas felt pain where the skin adhered to the plastic.

"Listen you little bugger, I won't be coming back in here again until feeding time. If you make another mess, you will just have to lay in it."

"Whhaaaaai." the sting of cold air on Elena's raw bottom along with a rough wipe of an already dirty diaper made the bawling even louder. The nurse flung the diaper into a pail in the corner. Then she took another rag and wiped the plastic with something that smelled of bleach and ammonia. When Elena's skin again contacted the still damp sheet, the burning became excruciating.

"Ahiiieeeeee," Elena wailed in pain.

"Would you quit the screaming? You're nine years old!" scolded the woman. "You'll never get out of this room and join the other children if you keep wailing like that… and certainly no one is going to want to take you home. Now just stop already! We have a group touring the orphanage this week from America, but nobody wants to visit a screaming child."

She pulled up the bars and reattached the duct tape restraint. "Whaaaaa," Elena immediately started her mournful cry. "Oh, shut up for once," the attendant said from the door. "What a waste you are. Sometimes I think it would have been better if you had never been born." She turned off the light, and as she closed the door uttered a curse, "Sweet Jesus, Elena you sure stink I'll be glad when you die, and I don't have to put up with your mess." Click, the door closed, plunging the room back into loneliness, bringing on more cries that died in the darkness.

Fear and pain overwhelmed Thomas. But now he remembered his out. "MYSWEETJE-SUS!" he uttered in desperation wanting to escape that dark prison.

Whoosh, the blackness turned to the gray mist.

Thomas, relieved to be back, collapsed before the beautiful Elena, "There has been a mistake," Thomas gasped. "What kind of madness did you take me to? That wasn't life! You sent me into a hell hole!"

"There has been no mistake," reassured Elena. Her serene presence quickly brushed aside the fear Thomas felt from his experience. "That was my life. I lived in Sighetu Orphanage, Northern Rumania."

"But, you?..." Thomas couldn't fathom how this peaceful, loving being came out of that hell. "Your mind and soul so shriveled from isolation and darkness. How could anything good come from that? I don't understand; your thoughts were so..."

"Disordered,... animalistic,... stunted,... I have heard many worse terms for what total neglect and isolation does to the brain, and yes, that happened and the damage was severe. I had no hope of any recovery, even with the best of care."

Elena smiled her wondrous smile and laughed, "Isn't God good?"

Recently experiencing Elena's harsh life, Thomas could not fathom calling God good. "No, it was horrible beyond description, and I worry going back there will drag me down into darkness instead of helping me to see. Please let me stay here with you forever, I don't want to ever go back there again."

Elena laughed, and love poured out like music. "Believe me, you don't want to stay here. My hug is but a taste, a faint echo of all that Jesus would have for you. His embrace far exceeds any pain that life could hold for us."

Thomas did not reply; he just wanted to drink in the moment and let it wash away the terror of Sighetu. Somewhere he had heard that name before.

Afraid of the Dark

Elena gave Thomas a hug and whispered, "We need to move on."

"You're not sending me back, are you?" Thomas pleaded. "Your life there is horrid and unending in its torture. But here, with you, there is not enough time to soak up the beauty you bring. Please, just let me stay here a little longer."

Elena held Thomas at arms length and looked him in the face.

"I cannot let you treat me as the final destination. I have nothing, and you will end up missing everything," she said. "My life on earth in all its horribleness made me greatly desire true life in Jesus. On earth I had no hope except God alone, and as you can see, He fulfilled it beyond my wildest dreams."

"Then take me to where my dreams can be fulfilled," said Thomas.

"Oh, Thomas, that is just the point. Your dreams and desires are about yourself. We all are a reflection of what we truly desire. Where your hope is placed will be the reflection of your life. You still have so much to learn."

"But I am afraid to go back, I have never felt so alone, so forgotten… The pain is just too much for me."

"Letting your fears direct you will only lead to darkness. It is a tool darkness uses to entrap and blind us from the real truth, but letting

God direct you in the darkness will lead you to His light."

"Truth?" questioned Thomas. "The truth is you had no life. I could hardly take it for a few minutes, let alone live it; I seriously wanted to die. You would have been better off dead…"

"How can you say that when you find such solace in my embrace," laughed Elena as she gave Thomas a hug that tingled with joy. "Would you prefer I not have lived—to not fulfill all this goodness? Even now my life is a gift from God, a gift to you for His good purpose."

"Forgive me," said Thomas looking up into her face brimming with goodness. "I spoke from …"

"Fear?… come, it is time to return," Elena said, placing her hand on his shoulder.

"Nooo, pleas…"

Whoosh.

Sweet Jesus

The pall of darkness greeted Thomas with the feeling of being lost and forgotten. The odor

of decay curled into his lungs like a snake, causing nauseating fright. No matter that he had recently seen Elena in all the radiance of heaven.
That vision quickly faded in the dankness of her
dungeon. Worst of all, the shroud of hopelessness, that no one cared, clung to everything with
the stench of rotting life. Elena struggled against
giving up—a great tug of war between life and
death. For his part Thomas could do nothing to
help, for he fought his own anguished battle over
remarks he had uttered numerous times during
his career—"this child would have been better if
they had never been born." Words that now made
him choke with shame.

"Whaaaaa," Elena cried out over and over.

For Thomas, chained with Elena in the
dark, the image of Elena's beauty and goodness
seemed an unreal dream—a cruel joke, not a
promise of heaven. The possibility of any future
snuffed out by the inky emptiness of the present.
Without hope, Elena had no prospect for a
blessed tomorrow, only the unrelenting pain of
the present stretching to the horizon. Any yearning by Elena for existence beyond the door of this
closet only made the current misery worse. Better

to not think of anything good and avoid the heightened torment of knowing that somewhere light shines, but you will never be able to partake in it. Darkness prevailed here—its claws sunk in too deep to allow any hope. The destruction of mind and body were severe and beyond ever getting better. Elena laid in filth held in place by duct tape, and nothing would change... ever... except through death. These malevolent thoughts also invaded Thomas' mind, and he, along with Elena, began to cry for the numbness of death. The only escape for those in darkness.

"Whaaaaaaaaaaaaaaaaa," she wailed.

Why continue with life? No one cares. Ugly thoughts dripped in a relentless stream upon Thomas. He felt himself being pulled down. The power of this gnawing despair made Thomas forget all that he had gone through: the brilliant light, meeting Joshua, and the beauty of Elena. It all became someone else's dream. Only endless darkness filled his vision with no hope of anything different—alone... alone... and forsaken.

"Whaaaaaaaaaaaaaaaaaa"

Thump... thump... thump, Thomas heard Elena's heart pound with her effort to survive.

How could she keep going? Soon a sinister presence hung over this little girl, spewing out ugliness. "Give up. It's no use. Why are you hanging on? No one cares." the voice clawed at the crib. Thomas focused his mind on Elena's heartbeat to keep from the fear and panic that swirled about with evil so close.

Elena drifted in and out of a restless sleep, but any noise would stir her pain and renew her crying.

"Whaaaaaaaa"

Thump... thump... thump went her heart, one beat after another.

During the sleep periods, Thomas watched Elena's dreaming. Usually, it swirled with nonsense, a relief from the misery of her reality. Though, sometimes into her sleep crept suffocating nightmares of torment that repeated over and over. These scared Thomas for he knew this to be the black hole calling to both of them, eroding the resolve to fight. Their desire to go on living teetered on the edge of a horrible dark abyss.

Thump... thump... thump.

It became difficult for Thomas to tell the difference between reality and dreams in the never ending darkness. He recognized that Elena had weakened, and her will to live wavered, growing more and more tired of the fight.

"Just let go," the voice whispered to Elena. The black hole opened its mouth before her. "Come in…" it beckoned, but Elena somehow fought back, hoping for light instead of succumbing to death.

Paradoxically, Thomas found himself desiring an end to this misery—the intoxicating promise of nothingness. *Get it over with. You can't go on like this. This life isn't worth another breath,* peppered Thomas' thoughts, and always in the background—"Come, I can give you relief. Don't fight it. You can rest in me." Thomas smelled the filthy rot but didn't care if it came from Elena, the dream, or the black hole. He couldn't take anymore and wanted out.

Thump… thump… thump.

Things appeared hopeless to Thomas, and he was about to call out "sweet Jesus," when something strange occurred. A musical chord pierced the gloom, causing a tear in the deep despair, letting a sliver of light into Elena's nightmare. Thomas couldn't tell if the music and light

were a dream or real. But Elena responded by trying to crawl toward the radiance, and a singer
joined the music: "Come My child. Let My love
hold you, let My hope surround you... I love you
and have good planned for you."

*How could this dream and a silly song do
anything for Elena's catastrophe of a life?* reasoned
Thomas. *Her brain has been severely damaged by
this place. She doesn't speak or even think rationally
let alone understand these words.* But, despite his
misgivings, the song awakened hope where there
was none. Thomas felt the yearning for life build
in Elena. Like water coming from a rock in the
desert, it brought hope that God cared for her.
Somehow Elena found respite from the taunting
darkness and strength to take another painful
breath. Bewildered, Thomas wondered, *What's
God up to?*

"Whaaaaaaa," Elena woke herself up crying
out.

Her cry touched something deep in
Thomas and ignited his anger. *That's it? God hands
out a few nice words in a dream to beat back all this
ugliness. And of course the predictable result is she
wakes up wailing in the dark. Elena's terrible life of*

fear, loneliness and growth stunting neglect requires more than some pretty words. Furious, Thomas wanted to quit, and almost blurted out "Sweet Jesus" as a curse, but something strange happened to stop him. That simple song in her dream had blossomed into a speck of goodness in Elena's bleak life—she really hoped to join in the song. A hope that had wilted in the cruelty of Sighetu and now coming to life giving her the desire to live. This dumbfounded Thomas for it had no rational explanation.

"Whaaaaaaa," thump... thump... thump. "Whaaaaaaa," thump... thump... thump... Ph-hhrrrrrt. The stink made Thomas want to throw-up. *I've had enough. I have to get out or I'll lose my mind. I don't know what keeps this little girl going, but it is not working for me.* "My sweet Jesus, get me out of here," he screamed, feeling guilty about leaving Elena in her wretchedness. But he didn't care; he only wanted to get away.

Whoosh.

Thomas inhaled deeply, like someone surfacing after nearly drowning. After a few gasps to calm down, he turned toward Elena to breathe in her loveliness. "I give up, I'll never understand your hope. It is impossible to live like that… I know it's beyond my capabilities. The hell you endured at Sighetu would have killed me had I not remembered—my sweet Jesus." Thomas cringed inside, knowing he had used the escape words more for a curse than anything else.

"You're closer than you realize," encouraged Elena. "You need to die to yourself, the good and the bad, before you can live to please my Jesus."

"What's the use," Thomas confessed. "I can't handle it. How will I survive going back to that place?"

"The question you should ask is how did I survive it? In the answer you will discover the hope your life is missing."

"I honestly don't know how…" Thomas didn't look at Elena knowing her beauty would only make him feel shame for taking the easy way out; his failure at not hanging in there to find the treasure she had discovered.

"Thomas," Elena said, putting her hand under his chin and raising his gaze till it met hers. Her gaze melted all his apprehensions. "Back there I received something that you missed, the first musical notes of heaven called hope."

"That was a dream," protested Thomas. "Hardly enough to combat the reality of your existence."

"That's where you are wrong," corrected Elena. "What seems impossible to endure in a world dominated by evil is possible by the Spirit of God. The right arm of God is not too short to save in any circumstance, and the beginning step is hope."

"But how did you find hope in God? It is an impossible leap in your broken state, especially when you have to wonder why God did that to you in the first place." Thomas felt an old anger toward God arise. How could He allow sickness and disease in children? "I spent my life giving hope to children. Where was God in all that?" Thomas said, turning his face away.

"My dear Thomas," said Elena. "Evil put me in that dark room, not God, but it is God who came and found me."

"Such suffering can hardly be turned around by a song in a dream," scoffed Thomas.

"I had nothing else to grab hold of. Hope in God looms large where there is no other hope to cling to," laughed Elena.

Thomas looked at Elena. She began to hum a single note, then she smiled, building the note into a beautiful symphony rich in life that made her even more beautiful, if that were possible.

You turned my wailing into dancing;
you removed my sackcloth and clothed me with joy,
that my heart may sing to you and not be silent.
O Lord my God, I will give you thanks forever.

The sweep of her song caught Thomas and lifted him to summits he never dreamed of. The wonder of going from so low to such great heights of goodness sent his heart and mind reeling. "The music is so exquisite here," exclaimed Thomas. "But I didn't hear it back on earth. If I would have heard it like you just sang, it would have made things different."

"That's what hope does—it makes things different," explained Elena. "Come, let's return to Sighetu. We are getting to the good part. It's where God used you in my life."

Elena's words triggered something in Thomas; his mind raced through memories of his medical career. Suddenly it dawned on him. "I remember now. I took nursing and medical students on tour to Rumania. We held a clinic at Sighetu. All the students found the condition of the children heartbreaking. Their needs were way beyond our ability to help in any meaningful way. Now, having experienced it from your point of view… I had no idea of the magnitude of the horror."

"Yes, I see you are beginning to understand," smiled Elena. "But the real help was not in what you considered meaningful."

"So our little one day clinic must have had a greater impact than I realized. It makes me feel good knowing I had a part in helping…"

As soon as these words slipped from the lips of Thomas, a loud belching sound rumbled through the gray mist.

Arrogant Death/179

Thomas shuddered at the sound of the dark abyss and gripped Elena's arm.

"Keep it away!" Thomas drew closer to Elena.

"Your pride provides a foothold for evil," said Elena. "When you claim glory for yourself instead of giving it to God, the lie you tell yourself will bring in more lies until your whole body is filled with ugliness and is only fit for the pit."

"Wait a minute, why do you call that a lie? As a doctor I have helped many people over the years, not just you. Give me some credit."

"Dear Thomas, the role you played in my life came about by God's doing, not yours. Furthermore, it is good that you helped people through medicine; that is not the problem. The lie comes in when you take credit for it instead of glorifying God. The beauty you see in me is not mine, but God's reflection in me. You can't reflect true glory when you keep getting in the way. Your life becomes a shadow rather than a beacon—a reflection of the darkness rather than the light."

"But…"

"Come, you have so much to learn." Elena placed her hand on Thomas before he could say more.

Whoosh.

A Song of Hope

"Whaaaaaaa."

Elena's scream submerged Thomas again into the utter hopelessness of Sighetu.

How will this hell teach me anything about light? Thomas thought. *There is no way out. Elena's body and brain are too scarred for any use. Her only hope is in death, not life.*

"Whaaaaaaa"

Thomas couldn't tell if the cry belonged to him or Elena, for the evil of Sighetu sucked a scream from everyone.

Help! Let me die. Thomas looked straight up at the ceiling. He felt cold, hungry and miserable with no end. Suddenly, the door opened and the fluorescent light flickered on, making Elena squint and cry even louder.

"They're here, Elena. Everyone gets a fresh bottom," said the middle-aged nurse with the red kerchief. She quickly took off the foul diaper, threw it in the pail and replaced it with a stained clean diaper. "You must behave when I bring them by; no crying. They need to see that we treat children well, though we are poor and over-burdened with work." She cut the duct tape off Elena's wrist with scissors and rubbed some ointment on the skin. "If you are good, I won't put the tape back on when they leave." Finally, she wiped the bed down with the bleach solution and left, leaving the light on and the door open.

Elena had never seen the door left open. When she heard the footsteps of a large group, she cried louder than ever, trying to get their attention.

"Whaaaaaa, whaaaaaa."

"This is Elena. She is quite difficult to handle even though her name means princess— that she is not." said the woman leading the tour. "Elena is nine but hasn't grown because of a glandular disorder. We placed her in this closet because she won't stop crying, and we don't want her to disturb the other children."

"Whaaaaaa, whaaaaaa," Elena gushed, pleading for help… anything to keep them there.

A familiar voice spoke up from the back of the crowd, "Take a look, but try not to disturb her. I am told she can get pretty loud."

Thomas winced when he recognized his own voice trying to steer the group away from Elena. *No, you fool. Let them stay. She is starving for attention; how can you treat her as a carnival creep show?*

"Keep moving; let everyone get a chance to see," intoned Dr Jones.

A number of students gawked through the door, holding surgical masks over their noses because of the room's stench.

"Olga!" said the person guiding the tour. "You forgot to empty the diaper pail. No wonder it stinks in here. Take it away now!"

Olga pushed her way through the crowd. "Scuze, scuze," she said. Part of the group had to move into the storage closet to make way for her to grab the bucket and leave.

"Using a closet for a room is not good, but we have no choice for our resources are small. We need more donations…" the woman droned on, trying to elicit funds.

"Whaaaaaaa"

"As I was saying, Elena never stops crying. If we had more money for staff…"

"Whaaaaaa"

Then over the bars of the bed a face appeared. Thomas looked up through Elena's eyes to meet the gaze of Becky, one of the nursing students. Her surgical mask dangled from her neck, letting the radiance of her smile bathe Elena in something she had never known before. With tears running down her cheeks, Becky reached into the crib and carefully lifted Elena up and held her close.

"I am not sure it is wise to touch or hold the children. There are any number of contagious diseases you might expose yourself to," said Dr. Jones from the rear of the students.

Thomas cringed at the sound of his voice. He wished he would shut up, for his words were distracting from the love being shown to Elena.

"Oh Elena, you are a sweet princess to Jesus," Becky cooed, drowning out all the other voices. Ignoring the smell and the warning, Becky encircled Elena with her arms and slowly began to hum, while rocking Elena. In Becky's warm embrace she stopped crying.

The wonder spread across Thomas as Elena rested from the horror of Sighetu. All five senses came alive with joy in that moment. Thomas recognized this joyful peace as similar to the comfort he received when Elena hugged him in the gray mist… it made life so precious and good.

Elena breathed easy, and for the first time in her life she experienced something other than loneliness and stifling darkness. Elena hoped this beautiful moment would last forever. Rocking back and forth enfolded in Becky's arms, Elena received a whispered blessing.

"Blessed are those who mourn, for they will be comforted."

Thomas knew that Elena couldn't possibly understand, but the sweetness that came with Becky's voice along with her actions conveyed the truth of what she said in a way that transcended Elena's mental disability and her lifetime of pain and hurt. Becky then started to sing, "Jesus loves you this I know…"

Thomas saw the heavens open and experienced a wonderful peace settle upon them. A heavenly chorus sang with Becky. The song of God's love for Elena. Thomas blissfully floated on each note letting the music wash over him. *How did I miss this?* he thought. *I don't recall this glorious music occurring when I led the students through Sighetu.* A startling conclusion hit Thomas—*this blessed moment eclipses anything I have ever done in medicine.* Another part of his mind quickly responded, *Don't be a fool. Elena is too traumatized to comprehend any of Becky's words let alone understand English. Why, this brief encounter of goodwill won't last, but my research will bless people for generations to come...*

"Jesus loves you this I know..." Becky sang.

Elena tried to imitate the lyrics. "Jes ov u..."

The feeble attempt shocked Thomas, who had heard nothing but incomprehensible wailing coming from Elena. *No! How can this be?... Her brain is too far gone. Elena can't make sense of anything.*

The song stirred the depths of Elena's soul. Spurred by her parched life she drank deeply of love. With all her might she crudely sang, and the joy of God blossomed in her barren life. "...*iss I nooo...*"

Skepticism continued to spoil the moment for Thomas as he wrestled with himself. *Why do I hold on to my doubt and disparage the hope Elena is receiving from a dumb children's song? Would I rob her of this for the appeasement of my intellect?* Then a thought popped into his mind—*Could it be that I have been blinded to love by my success?*

Words do not come close to describing this moment in Elena, for in the deepest part of her soul she now knew what she had been crying for... the love of Jesus and hope that comes with His love. Thomas, finally overcome with emotion, began to weep with joy. For his soul had been thirsty too, and he did not realize what it was till now. *I want what Elena has been given.*

The song touched Elena's heart, lifting her in hope to see the glorious light of heaven. No thought of darkness, no place for despair, just peace and joy.

The voice of Dr. Jones broke into heaven's love song. "Let's not waste anymore time here — we have much to observe and do before the bus comes to pick us up."

Thomas screamed at himself, "No... no... don't you understand, this embrace is glorious. Don't cut it off!"

"Becky, time to go. Put the little girl down in her crib and let's move on. Oh, and make sure you use this sanitizer. We'll change your clothes back at the hotel. Until then, don't touch anything."

Becky's arms trembled as she carefully lowered Elena into the crib. Immediately, Elena started to cry, "Whaaaaa." As the students left, someone remarked, "Well, Becky, a lot of good that did."

Becky stopped, looked straight at her detractor and with a quavering voice responded, "Well, at least for five minutes she wasn't crying. Jesus loves her too, you know."

As the door to Elena's room closed and darkness settled in, Thomas noted a difference in Elena's cry. Before, the cry summoned thoughts of fear, pain, and being abandoned. Now it expressed the hope to be held again by love. The darkness didn't hold the same terror; the loneliness lost some of its bite; the tedium was broken by expectation. Becky's embrace had awakened in Elena a hope of something outside these bars and walls—something to fill the aching void in her soul. Elena experienced love, and now she wanted more. Oh, the sweet embrace of Jesus—the hope of glory, of peace, and beauty beyond comprehension.

This glorious moment swept up Thomas in an epiphany of wonder where he couldn't help but utter—"my sweet Jesus!"

Whoosh.

Back in the gray mist Thomas looked at Elena, her radiance shown with goodness that sparkled in the reflection of the one in whom she hoped.

"I am surprised," said Thomas. "How can so much come from so little? A nursing student holds you and sings a children's song, and everything changes? I don't get it."

"That is the power of hope in God—the marvelous miracle of Jesus," said Elena. "Becky's embrace wasn't simply five minutes of being held. What I received was the embrace of a loving God. Just like my embrace is not mine but a reflection of Him. Does it not awaken in you a longing to be carried in His arms forever?"

"Yes…" Thomas said.

"Little things become profound miracles in Jesus." Elena beamed, and an exquisite warmth tumbled through Thomas.

"I still have a question," asked Thomas. "Why all the suffering?"

"I can only tell you that my life in Him more than makes up for all I went through. It is so huge that it has changed my weeping into rejoicing, and I would not want it any other way," Elena said smiling.

"The old 'pie-in-the-sky,'" Thomas said with a twinge of condescension. "If I had had that attitude, I would never have worked so hard to alleviate suffering. Just let'm wait for the sweet bye and bye."

"I think you are missing the point. Of course people should strive to ease suffering. You experienced how much that embrace from Becky helped me. She became Jesus to me. That song gave me hope."

"But God should have done more," protested Thomas.

"No, you see it as insignificant because you judge by what earns the applause of mankind rather than what is glorious in heaven. Decide for yourself, did Becky's embrace transcend the hell of Sighetu?"

Elena's aura seemed to pulse with intensity, and Thomas had to shield his eyes from her beauty. She smiled, and music danced around Thomas with the wonderful fragrance of goodness. *Mmmm,* his mind floated on each note until Thomas could not hold back from thinking—*oh my, how sweet is Jesus.*

Dying from Anger

Thomas watched Elena dance and sing for quite some time. In it he could taste, see, and hear the wonders of being in the presence of God. It made Thomas desire to join her in such won-

derful praise. Yet, he knew he couldn't. His awkward attempt would be a distraction rather than
as a participant; spoiler of beauty rather than a
part of it. This praise and worship of God by Elena had strength and richness that lifted his spirit
to places he had never thought possible, but
along with the rapture of seeing Elena's rejoicing
came sadness, for he knew it would go on without him. The prospect of being left out of such
rejoicing stirred remorse as great as the joy he
now beheld. In that knowledge, he withdrew into
sullen contemplation of his own dismal life, or
rather the lack of it.

Finishing her swirling dance before the
Lord, Elena looked at Thomas sulking in the
mist. "Thomas, your spirit is downcast because
you continue to look at yourself instead of focus-
ing on the Lord's majesty. I want to show you
how God used that five-minute embrace from
Becky and miraculously blessed it for all eternity."

Elena placed her hand on Thomas. He
took a breath, not sure what to expect, but
earnestly desiring to know more. Deep within, he
began hoping for hope.

Whoosh.

Once again Thomas entered Elena's life. This time curious to see this grand blessing played out. To his surprise, the dark room still felt suffocating, and it had the same detestable odor of hopelessness. Not a temporary soon-to-be-over odor, but a never ending, no chance of escaping odor. Disappointment filled Thomas for he expected to see some miraculous transformation of Elena, not the same forsaken and neglected existence.

"Nothing has changed!" Thomas cried out. "God, if I am to hope in You then show me Your power. If You remain silent, I will be dragged down into this pit of hopeless despair."

Thump… thump… thump, Elena's heartbeat continued.

Deep within Elena, an inner voice sang between the beats of her heart. "Jesus loves me this I know… thump, Jesus loves me this I know… thump, Jesus loves me this I know." These simple repeated words took root in Elena's heart, driving out the hopelessness of Sighetu. Infused throughout echoed the Bible verse:

"Blessed are they who mourn, for they will be comforted."

Comforted…blessed, These sounds rolled through Elena, and the sweetness of heaven descended on her soul. Thomas saw comfort and hope replacing her bleakness. *Still, I don't see how this could turn Elena into the beautiful person I met in the gray land.*

"Jaus wove ma es no…" Elena's voice struggled to make music. "Jaus wove ma thes aa no"

Elena's attempt to mimic Becky shocked Thomas, for he had only heard her wail in the past. She worked and worked to get her lips and tongue to move right, to carve out notes of music where screaming and yelling had ruled. He could feel Elena's heart longing to rise with each guttural effort. Still, the years of abuse and neglect kept dragging her back down.

Thomas continued to struggle with doubt. *Look at her, alone, restrained to the crib with duct tape, the burn of dirty diapers waiting to be changed, that's Elina's reality. How is trying to sing a dumb children's song going to change anything?*

"Jeus ove miiii…."

Thump… thump… thump.

Thomas began to see those three words glow deep within Elena. Like a beacon in the night—a point upon which Elena fixed her thoughts and hopes, allowing her to endure the pain. She repeated the lyrics over and over. Surprisingly, they never lost their luster. In fact, with each repetition, they grew in radiance and depth and power.

"Jesu wooooove me es I knoooowwww…" slowly pushed in between her fits of crying.

These words even began to affect Thomas. *Jesus loves me? Is that possibly true for…*

Suddenly the door opened. "What are you crying about now?" Olga cursed at Elena. "Time for your dinner. Though I should beat you, not feed you, for how you behaved in front of our guests the other day. Your screaming got me into big trouble. I should let you starve and be rid of you. That doctor complained to the supervisor about letting you scream all the time. Then, when that nursing student held you, the doctor fussed you might have something contagious."

"Jesu wooooove me es I knoooowwww... Ahkkkkkk...Jesu wooooove me es I knoooowwww...whaaaaaa."

"O shut up. My job is in jeopardy because of you." She propped a grungy blanket under Elena's head to allow her to feed.

"Jesu ooooove miii thsss I knooowww."

"Elena, stop, your caterwauling; it's driving me crazy," complained Olga.

Elena kept trying to sing, feeling more hopeful with each note.

"Jesu wove me es I knooow." Elena's voice stumbled over the words.

Then it struck Olga, "Why Elena I do believe you are attempting to sing." She laughed in surprise that Elena could do anything beyond whining. "Maybe we should take you to perform at the opera house in Bucharest."

When Elena opened her mouth to sing again, Olga shoved in some mush.

"Ha, tricked you didn't I," Olga chuckled.

Half the mush tumbled back out and down her chin. Elena coughed, seeking to clear her airway.

"What song are you singing?" For the first time Olga's voice softened, and she seemed genuinely interested in Elena.

"Jesu wooooove me es I knoooowwww, cough, Jesu wooooove me es I knoooowwww…"

"I know, it is that song that American student sang to you. 'Isus mă iubeşte,' It has been a long time since I last heard it…" Olga grew somber as she thought back to her childhood. "My mother used to sing that song for me each night before bed, and I sang it to my daughter before she…"

"Jesu ove mă, es I no… Jesu ove me, es I no," Elena continued to repeat.

"You don't even know what that song means," said Olga as she lifted some more mush in a serving spoon to Elena's tiny mouth. "I remember my Crina singing that song…" Olga trailed off into deep thought as tears formed in her eyes. She paid little attention to feeding, and the spoon missed Elena's mouth. Some food got on Elena's cheek, some on her nose, and the rest tumbled down her neck.

Olga laughed to hide the pain, "Just look at you. Food on your face. You can hardly eat. You can only eat and poop—you're hardly human. Why would you try to sing, and why that song?"

"Jesu ove me, I knooo…"

Olga's demeanor suddenly turned sour. "Your limbs all contorted, your body small and sickly, your brain is like this bowl of mush… no one wants you… who could ever love you?… why are you still alive?… Jesus doesn't love anyone. It's all a big lie. You don't know anything, but I know that song is a bunch of useless words."

"Jesus oves me, es…"

Olga cursed as she grabbed Elena's blanket from under her head and raised her shaking fist toward the ceiling. "Is this what you do, destroy people? What kind of God are you?"

Sobbing, she shook the blanket at God, raining down crumbs of mush upon the crib. "God why did you let my little Crina die, yet You let this defective one live? It makes no sense… The song speaks of your love—yet we have nothing but misery! This one would be better off dead, not my Crina."

"Jesu loves me…" Elena held on to this one song, but the darkness continued to tear at both of them.

"God doesn't care," said a low voice from the shadows. Then strangely Olga repeated it as if it were her own words. "God doesn't care about you," Olga spit the words at Elena.

"A broken, messed up piece of garbage, a worthless smudge of humanity that should be thrown away." Suffocating anger and bitterness spewed across the room. The ugly words coloring everything with the wretchedness of hell.

"Jesu loves me…" Elena's voice cracked with the effort. "Jesus loves me…."

"Where are you God?" Thomas yelled, feeling powerless to stop the downward spiral. "Why do you let hell have its way with these two poor souls? Do something!"

"Jesus love me, Dis I knoow," Elena sang.

In a fit of rage, Olga brought the blanket down to cover the face of Elena to stop her from singing the words that caused such pain.

"Aiiieee." Elena felt panic as she struggled to breathe.

"Shut up! Just shut up! Would you stop singing," cried Olga as she pushed harder on the blanket covering Elena.

In Elena's fight for air, Thomas saw something astounding—this poor miserable child wanted life. She hated the darkness and desolation of her life, but she didn't want to die. Rather, she wanted to live—to love and be loved. A fulfillment of her deepest hopes and dreams. Even though her body and mind were damaged beyond hope of repair, Elena's spirit hoped, not for death, but for life far exceeding the walls of the closet.

"Help meee Jesu…" A muffled prayer escaped from under Olga's hand.

Sensing eminent death, Thomas screamed, "She can't breathe, she can't breathe. Lord do something!" He lost control and panicked.

Elena squirmed, trying to twist free, but lacked the strength, and she began to fade.

We're going to die, thought Thomas.

Thump….thump……….thump…………
..thump

Help....help.......help.........hel...

Thomas fought with Elena to breathe, and with their waning strength, the sadness became overpowering. *What a shame.* Thomas remembered talking with Elena in the gray mist about how God could bless the brief comfort of a nursing student into so much more. *Is this supposed to glorify God? Disability is not glorious. Child abuse is not glorious. Murder is not glorious. Dying alone and forgotten is not glorious. God, how did you let this happen?* Thomas couldn't see anything for the dirty blanket pressing hard against Elena's face. The darkness had won.

Ever so faint, Thomas thought he heard the sound of rushing wind, and a softening of Olga's hand pushing down on Elena. A fragrant aroma came in with the wind, like morning dew in a forest glade. The sweetness pushed back the foul odor, and an inexplicable peace settled upon everything.

Is she dying? thought Thomas.

As the darkness retreated, Elena relaxed.

What is going on? The light grew with intensity till Thomas recognized it as the same glow he had seen in the gray lands that burned when he had tried to approach. *The light's not burning me!*

God's glorious presence filled the room and filled Elena. A deep rumbling rolled through the air forming words that broke like waves upon Elena and Olga, "Elena and Crina are My children, much adored, and most precious in my sight."

The sound surprised Olga making her stop pressing her hand over Elena's face. She looked around for the source only to see Elena's tiny hand protruding from under the blanket. "What have I done?" Olga cried out in fear. "Oh, sweet Jesus," she wailed, suddenly realizing the horrible act coming from her sorrow. Quickly pulling the blanket back, she uncovered Elena's face. "Elena! Please, Elena, breathe. Don't let her die… Lord have mercy!… Oh my God, forgive me… Please God, help Elena to live," Olga cried as she bent over and cradled Elena in her arms. Weeping and rocking, Olga prayed with the fervor of a desperate mother—pleading for heaven's healing. "I am a bitter old woman filled with pain. Please Lord, give breath back to Elena… breathe life into my darkness."

The room filled with light and love and joy in a wonderful sweet aroma that Thomas knew now as the embrace of Jesus. The same glorious passion he had experienced when Becky held Elena, and Elena held him. *O Lord, thank You,* exclaimed Thomas.

Olga cried out, "Forgive me for my bitterness toward You. Wash me in Your mercy." She felt the weight on her heart ease as she became swept up into the lap of God. She did not fully understand, but knew the Lord's arms wrapped around her and Elena with a brilliance of light, music and love. In that moment, Olga's anger with the Almighty melted in His embrace.

Elena took a big breath and then another.

The beauty now unfolding from this frail, deformed little girl had touched Olga helping to heal deep wounds of grief, to give hope where none existed. A miraculous healing of her spirit, new life where death and hopelessness once ruled. The magnitude of such a miracle exceeded Thomas' ability to fully comprehend. He only knew that through Elena's mangled life, God brought forth His glory in a way that upended anything this world could offer.

"I want to be part of that," longed Thomas.

An intense light bathed the room holding Thomas in rapt attention.

"Elena, My child," a voice gushed from the light like a mighty waterfall. "I am not ready to take you home. There is more I wish to do with your life. Though you mourn for a little while, hang on to your hope in Me, the glory will be so worthwhile."

The brilliance subsided, leaving a tingling in the air.

"Cough..." came from Elena's flaccid body, and a bit of mush drooled down her chin.

Olga looked at Elena, her tiny chest rising and falling. With great relief Olga began to weep uncontrollably, "Thank you Jesus, thank you... You have stopped my hand from evil, and by saving this child you have saved me. You have given me life and hope where darkness reigned." Then she leaned over and kissed Elena on the forehead, and from her lips came a mother's song,

"Jesus loves you—loves you still,
though you're weak and very ill;
from his shining throne on high,
He comes to watch you where you lie."

She held Elena for a long time, gently rocking back and forth, singing to Elena.

Finally Olga looked up and prayed, "Jesus, I don't fully understand, but as I hold Elena, I know You are even now embracing my Crina. Forgive me for doubting Your love. Though I miss Crina, I know she is in Your care just like Elena."

Looking at Olga through Elena's eyes, Thomas beheld the joy of heaven in her tears of joy.

Olga finished feeding Elena and put her back into the crib.

Immediately Elena screeched out her song, "Jesu, oves me…"

Olga paused at the door, turned and prayed, "Thank you Jesus for the hope and love you have given Elena, and now through her You have blessed me with the hope of Your glory."

As Thomas looked up at the bars of the crib, "my sweet Jesus" slipped from him like a prayer.

Whoosh.

Silly Song

Back in the gray mist, Thomas looked at Elena. "I don't know what to say. Back there with Olga... the embrace of heaven changed Olga from trying to kill you in a fit of rage to holding you in love. How? You were in such utter poverty and desolation at every level... It strains credulity that such a radical transformation could take place..."

"Just as you find it hard to believe that from my tortured existence the life you see before you can arise, so you now find it difficult to believe Olga could be lifted from the darkness of her own soul. What is impossible for us is possible with God."

As Thomas gazed at Elena, her beauty seemed even more radiant than he remembered, if that were possible. He had to squint, but refrained from shielding his eyes. "I want what you have," he blurted out. "But..."

"But something holds you back," replied Elena.

Thomas averted his gaze. "I can't get past the fact that it all just seems too good to be true. Life isn't some fairytale—'and they all lived happily ever after.'"

"You are your biggest obstacle to truly seeing and believing," said Elena. "You rely on your own judgement as to how life should be. You give no credence to the love of God at work in His creation. How can you see when you denigrate what God is doing because it doesn't follow your expectations? Even now, I stand before you, a new creation in Jesus. Still you refuse to see. Instead, you continue holding onto the foolish intelligence of a fallen world, despite what you have witnessed in Joshua and me. Furthermore, you treat as a myth the death and resurrection of Jesus and thus deny its power to give life where there is none. And now, even as I embrace you with the love of God, you cannot release yourself into it. Thomas, unless you allow yourself to be a fool for heaven, that pride of yours will be the death of you."

"I…" stammered Thomas

Elena continued, "There it is again, your pride creating a barrier to Jesus. You label things as below your intelligence and elevate yourself unto the throne of life. We only reflect what we worship," Elena continued. "For your entire life you have worshiped intellect, talent and human beauty, but over time they will decay and collapse and you along with them. You need to worship God, putting your hope and faith in Him. Then true goodness does not depend on your ability or effort but upon the mercy of God in Jesus, who will never see decay. What you see in me is the result of God's miraculous goodness."

"But…"

Elena put her finger to Thomas' lips. "No more 'buts,'" she said. "Let me instead show you one last miracle of God."

Whoosh.

Thomas tumbled back into the same foul smelling crib and dark room tucked somewhere in the bowels of Sighetu Orphanage.

How is this worth anything? thought Thomas. *The dreariness in this place, if anything, feels worse. Has anything changed?*

Elena's mind occupied itself by humming over and over the only song she knew, four bars of "Jesus Loves Me."

It surprised Thomas that this song still held Elena's attention, "Doesn't she ever get tired of it?" A sudden pang of guilt struck him as he remembered Elena's remarks about his pride and labeling things as foolish and below his intelligence.

Eventually Elena drifted into sleep. Her mind swirled with disjointed images: Olga, the bars of the crib, what it would be like to walk out in the light. But, dominating all these thoughts stood the vision of Becky smiling and sweetly singing, "Jesus loves me, this I know…"

"She still is just waiting to die. What kind of life is that?" Thomas thought. Then he noticed a vile odor seeping through the room, making it hard to breathe. Undisturbed, Elena's dreams revolved around the song.

Thomas's mind switched to a question that troubled him. *How did Elena come to understand these words? She doesn't have the capacity to know more than a few words of Rumanian, let alone the English Becky sang.* The question only heightened the mystery over the miracle happening in this forgotten closet to a useless little girl. *I'll have to ask Elena. If I can remember.* He realized that her beauty made him forget a lot of things.

"For the Bible tells me so…" Elena's dreaming repeated over and over.

In any other circumstance this would be boring beyond endurance, Thomas thought. *But here, there is nothing… nothing to hold on to, nothing to brighten Elena's day, I guess it serves a purpose.* He laughed to himself, thinking of a quote from Karl Marx: *"religion… is the opiate of the masses." Certainly that is the case here.* A sudden twinge of guilt touched him concerning the worship of the world's intelligence.

The hours seemed like years to Thomas in the cold desolate life of Elena. After the millionth verse of "Jesus loves me," Thomas noted a faint spot of warmth taking hold in Elena. *What could this be? So strange that in a place so devoid of everything except tedium punctuated by pain, her life could produce anything good because of a few words.* As the wonder unfolded and developed, Thomas realized what now occupied a prominent place in Elena. Hope!

Every time Olga came into the room she would pick up Elena and sing, "Jesus loves me…"

Though initially faint, Elena's hope grew with wonderful dreams of being held and sung to. Thomas saw it touch and warm every part of Elena. How amazing, thought Thomas, where there is nothing, love's whisper can blossom and grow into such passionate hope. Now, instead of the fetid smell of filth, Thomas breathed in the scent of heaven and realized an amazing transformation had begun. The once shriveled spirit of Elena swelled with the love of God.

"Yes, Jesus loves me… Yes, Jesus loves me…"

Rumble… pfffffft… pooffffiiit. Elena's bowels let loose their contents.

With a start, Elena awoke. The darkness growled in a fiendish effort to derail Elena's dream by causing a vile discharge. Her diaper overflowed with stool that dragged Elena back to the reality of her dark putrid closet. Thomas felt a thickness in the air that pulled at each breath. The smell grew to stifling proportions in an attempt to bury her hope with the wretchedness of Sighetu.

"You are no good," said a voice from the shadows. "A waste of time. No one wants you. You've messed your bed, and that is all you are good for—waiting for someone to clean up your poop."

The fingers of darkness seemed to tighten around Elena. She began to choke with fear mixed with the smell... *I can't breathe, I can't breathe!*

Again the voice of darkness pushed at Elena. "You don't even love yourself—how could Jesus love you. It's all a lie." The grip tightened, trying to snuff out all hope.

Suddenly from beyond the door came the song, "Little ones to Him belong. They are weak but He is strong." Piercing the darkness, the music had its own power, far greater than Thomas had thought possible with a children's song. "Yes, Jesus loves me." The words bludgeoned the darkness. "I may be weak, but He is strong," Elena's spirit warmed with each note and the darkness fell back.

Suddenly the door opened. The light made Elena squint, but she loved it, for with it came fresh air and Olga.

"Yes, Jesus loves me... Oh my, Elena, what's that smell." Olga said as she stepped into the room. "You poor dear, I'll get you cleaned up."

With quick efficiency Olga cleaned off Elena, changed her diaper and wiped down the bed. All the while, singing her own verses to "Jesus Loves Me."

"Jesus loves me, this I know,
Though in life I struggle so.
My hope in Him holds me near,
By His love that drives out fear.
Yes, Jesus loves me..."

Thank you, Jesus, Thomas thought as Olga sang.

Elena smiled in the light.

"Elena, I have a surprise for you," said Olga. "You're getting out of here. I got permission to move you back to my ward. I told the supervisor you wouldn't scream anymore, just a little singing. Besides, they need this room for supplies that the last tour group left to the orphanage. Oh, and one more surprise, remember Becky, the girl who held you and sang for you. She left you a

Rumanian Bible. In it she had the translator write: 'to Elena, God's lovely child.' I'll read some verses to you after we get you moved."

Olga put the Bible down next to Elena and began moving the bed through the door. One wheel, stuck with rust, causing the whole thing to veer to the left, scraping the door-jamb with a terrible screech. It scared Elena, and she started to cry. Immediately, Olga stopped pushing the crib and lifted Elena into her arms.

"Isus mă iubeşte…" Olga's voice brought with it a joyful peace that soon enwrapped Elena in a heavenly embrace.

Thomas couldn't help but give in to the song and allowed himself to be swept up in the glorious hope of Elena.

I love You, Jesus, welled up in Elena and spilled over into Thomas.

"Yes, Jesus loves me…" Thomas found himself joining in. The contrast of being alone in the stinking dark, to being held in the light brought such joy and hope, he could hardly believe it.

I wonder, mulled Thomas, *maybe the joy and hope in God is proportional to the need and desire.*

"O Thomas won't you stop analyzing everything and just enjoy, this moment," a voice thundered in Thomas' soul… and he obeyed.

Olga finally maneuvered the crib into a ward with nine other children all closely packed with only a small open area at the door where a single chair-desk stood. Three windows along one wall let in light through glass that had years of dirt. One pane had a crack covered with masking tape. The walls were painted white; the floor checkered with white and red tiles, and overhead fluorescent lights illuminated the room. One light flickered trying to hold on to life… or death, depending on your point of view. Elena enjoyed being with others. In the bed across from hers, a boy stood holding onto his crib rail staring at her. He had tape restraints on each ankle to keep him from climbing out. His face had a blank, lifeless expression as he chewed on his lower lip. Thomas wondered how many of the orphans were like him, minds permanently damaged, each becoming little unreachable islands.

"Okay Elena, this is your new home," said Olga. "Like I promised, I will read to you from your Bible. Becky wrote a note for you. I think it says, 'Jesus loves you' then a verse, Matthew 19:14, Jesus said, 'Let the little children come to me, and do not hinder them...'"

When Olga closed the Bible, she noticed Alex, the boy standing in the next crib, staring at them. "Well, Alex, did you like the verse too?"

Alex just stood in his crib and stared.

"Elena, why don't we sing your song for Alex," Olga said. She picked up Elena and carried her over to Alex.

"Jesus loves me! This I know,
For the Bible tells me so;
Little ones to him belong;
They are weak, but He is strong."

As the song tumbled out of Elena and Olga, Thomas realized Elena's hope had grown from something small to blessing Olga with hope for her Crina, and now even hope for Alex. So they sang and sang, but the boy's expression did not change, he just stared and bit his lower lip.

"Elena, I must take you around and introduce you to the other children," Olga said. "This is Alex. Unlike you he doesn't make a sound, so I think you two will make up for each other's temperament." Olga laughed and she gave Elena an extra hug. Then she reached an arm around Alex and tried to give him a hug, but he only stiffened and pushed away.

Elena looked at Alex and began to sing again. "Jesu ove me…"

The intensity of Elena's feelings toward Alex surprised Thomas. She seemed to be calling to him with a power greater than anything he had felt in her before. For a moment, Thomas saw a flicker of something in Alex's eyes, like something trying to awaken, but then it was gone.

Olga moved on, "Next to Alex is Nadia, she is…"

"Aaaaaa," cried Alex.

"Why Alex," laughed Olga, "This is a surprise, I have never heard you make a sound before." She returned to Alex's crib.

Elena's emotions surged with hope for Alex. "Jesu oves you," she fumbled through the words, more screeching than singing, trying to reach out and touch this boy.

Olga felt Elena squirm in her arms toward Alex. "Oh, Elena, I think you want to give Alex a hug." Olga said, bringing Elena closer to Alex.

Alex stood there, but this time when Olga gently put her arm on him, he stopped biting his lip and made a squeak of delight.

Thomas shared Elena's thrill in the hug of those three. Wonderful hope poured forth from heaven in a joyous wave of glory that moved Olga to tears of joy.

Elena looked up into Olga's face, "Jesu ove you."

"Yes, Jesus loves me," whispered Olga. "I love you, Elena, and I love Alex." Olga leaned over and kissed Elena then Alex.

Alex's eyes grew wide, and tears started to run down his cheeks. "Jesu oves," his little voice squeaked

Olga gasped, "Alex, you talked!"

"Jesu oves you, Jesu oves you," Elena said, bursting with joy.

At this point, the children on the ward started banging on their cribs, for they too wanted Elena to sing for them.

"Elena, looks like you are popular. Everyone seems to want your attention," Olga said, as she looked around the room. "Come on, I will introduce you to each one. We can sing your song and give each a hug."

Olga took Elena around to the other cribs, calling out each name as if announcing their arrival at a heavenly celebration just for them. Some children shook the bars to let Olga know that they wanted to be picked up too. At each bed Olga sang with Elena, "Jesus loves me this I know…" Olga even sang some verses she had made up: "Jesus loves me though I roam, He will come and lead me home." But there was one verse Olga sang that made Elena shriek with joy, "Jesus wants you for His own, to be your comfort when you groan."

After Olga had taken Elena around to meet the other orphans, she took her back to her own crib and laid her down. The sound of children all around trying to sing made Olga smile.

Thomas experienced in each encounter the wonderful embrace of heaven and breathed in the fragrant glory of each child. *Who would have believed this joy tumbling about,* thought Thomas. *All because Becky embraced Elena and sang for her a simple children's song.*

That night when the lights went off, Elena looked out between the bars and smiled. The joy of meeting each child continued to wash over her.

Thomas enjoyed it too and felt more alive than he had ever felt before. It struck him that Elena's life had brought more joy and goodness in this one day at Sighetu Orphanage than all his medical expertise. "What a difference hope can bring into life," he sighed.

The ward settled into coughs and snores, which were like music to Elena after years in the closet. But as the night progressed, an ominous foreboding filled the air. Thomas recognized this evil. It came from the dark closet, searching to reclaim and take back what had been taken from it. The darkness in the ward gathered strength, and Thomas could sense it gathering around Elena.

"Worthless," growled a voice out of the dark. "You think a stupid children's song can do anything to make up for being an ugly mistake— a blight upon humanity." The voice slithered under the bed. Surprisingly, the voice appeared to recognize Thomas' presence in Elena.

"What do you want?" challenged Thomas. "Be gone. Jesus loves Elena."

"You are hardly one who can toss around that name. You have used it more for mockery than anything else. Don't you think it's a bit hypocritical for you to use that name now?"

Elena continued a restless sleep along with the rest of the children. All except Alex, who stood quietly, eyes wide, staring at the thing below Elena's crib.

"I'll show everyone what happens when they try to escape." The growl turned to a gurgling. "She is mine!"

A sharp sensation dug into Elena's back. She arched and tried to scream, but her jaw clenched tight. Every muscle in her body started to spasm and cramp with horrible pain. Alex screamed when he saw Elena begin to shake uncontrollably. Her eyes rolled back, limbs shaking the air, and the crib began to bounce. The muscles in Elena's chest squeezed down, forcing out all the air.

I can't breathe, I can't breathe, Jesus help me, ran through Elena's mind.

Fear filled Thomas. "Sweet Jesus, help us," he shouted, expecting to be whooshed back to the gray mist, but nothing happened. Death's grip only tightened, as the darkness continued in rage, twisting around her little body until it squeezed and contorted Elena, causing her to vomit and flood her airway.

"Mine, mine, mine," the darkness bellowed.

"Yes, Jesus loves me… yes, Jesus loves me," squeaked the little voice of Alex.

"MINE!" shouted the voice, and it was over. Death released its hold. The job complete. The convulsing ceased as urine and stool flowed over Elena's crib. Her body lay still and unbreathing.

Thomas found himself no longer in Elena, but floating above as an observer. A serene heavenly calm came, expanding into all the space of that ward. Thomas saw Elena's soul stand up in her crib and a beautiful glow illuminated her face.

"I love you Elena." A sweet voice came from above.

"Oh Jesus, I love you," Arose like a song from Elena.

"Elena, I choose you to be with me forever."

"You… You want me?…" asked Elena

"Yes, so very, very much,"

A fragrant aroma filled the air, driving out the filth and fear of the dark hole.

"You are so beautiful Elena; all heaven awaits you."

"Oh my sweet Jesus," Elena said. "I want you with all my heart."

Alex stared at Elena, and tilted his head to listen, as her heavenly voice filled the room.

"Jesus loves me! He who died.
Heaven's gate to open wide;
He will wash away my sin,
Let His little child come in."

Alex stood transfixed by the light that surrounded Elena, then she was gone.

The light turned to Alex and said, "Elena is with me now. Nothing more can hurt her. I want you to know I love you too, Alexander. Someday, I will come and bring you home with Me. Until then, continue to hope in Me. You are very special in my sight."

The light left and Alex started to sing, "Jesus loves me this I know…"

The door burst open with the night attendant coming to see why all the commotion. When she saw Elena's limp body covered with feces, she gasped. "Sweet Jesus, what has happened."

Whoosh.

The Purpose of Life

Thomas fell exhausted onto the rough ground in the gray mist, his mind still shaking from witnessing Elena's death. Two hands lifted him to his feet.

"It's okay," reassured Elena. "God did not let evil have the last word in my life; instead, he wove each moment, good and bad, into the beauty you see before you. My hope sustained me then and has been fulfilled in Him for all eternity."

"But the darkness killed you with that seizure; it took your life just as you were having some purpose," Thomas protested.

"Purpose? My purpose is to glorify God. How God chooses to do that is up to Him, not you or me. I put my hope in the Lord, that's all I could do. Jesus took my name Elena, which means 'princess' and did more than I could ever imagine. I am His glorious princess," She twirled like a little girl showing off her new dress. God allowed me to sing for Him shining light in that dark place—"And now, Sighetu's darkness will never touch me again."

"The power of evil turned around by hope?" questioned Thomas.

"Not turned around… it was destroyed. I rejoice in what I went through, for God used it in amazing ways. My hope in Jesus spread to Olga, Alex, and the entire orphanage. A hope for God's goodness and glory that far out weighs all the suffering." Elena smiled and started to sing:

"Death ruled and had me chained,
shrouded in the awful dark,
But hope in His unfailing love,
lit a humble spark.
At first a smoldering wick—
hope burning gainst the night.
Jesus' mighty love the fuel,
made my hope grow ever bright.
With faith in His unfailing love,
Oh, what a wondrous sight.
shining forth till it leads me home,
Hope, the light of life."

Thomas had often put down such thinking as religious hogwash. A feeble effort to cover over suffering in the world. But standing here, in the presence of such beauty and goodness, made his past arguments look foolish. God's ability to take the worst situation and make it into heaven's glory left Thomas speechless. How wrong he had been to place his hope in earthly things and neglect the heavenly.

Attempting to change the conversation, Thomas inquired, "Dare I ask what happened to Alex?"

Elena smiled, "He has become quite the singer. I hope someday you will come with me to hear him sing."

Thomas' heart skipped with the word hope. "I would like that very much," he said.

"Then let your hope in God fill to over-flowing."

"But, I am not sure that God would honor my hope, since I have never hoped in Him before."

"That certainly sounds logical, except, that is not how it works with Jesus. 'A bruised reed He will not break, a smoldering wick He will not put out.' I had no hope until Becky sang to me, but when I listened to the words, I knew Jesus loved me. That is what my hope is built upon." With that Elena turned and started to sing as she walked away, "Jesus loves me, this I know for the Bible tells me so…"

Thomas watched her disappear into a brilliant dawn that forced him to look away. When he looked again the drab gray mist had returned. Immediately Thomas tried to discern the direction he should go to follow Elena, but everything looked the same—gray blending into nothing.

He longed to be with her, to feel the joy of her presence.

"Elena, come back," shouted Thomas. "I want to go with you."

His words fell silent in the mist. Thomas knew Elena would scold him—"It is not about me, it's about Jesus." That scared him, for the name Jesus called into question the value of his life's work; a career he still considered good and worthy of heaven. Struggling to hold on to some memory of Elena, he kept repeating the vision of her singing, "Jesus loves me this I know…" Sprinkling in her last words to him: "I knew Jesus loved me, that is what my hope is built upon." Those words, 'Jesus loves me,' held great joy if you believed them to be true. But not seeing Elena with her beauty, his old doubts began to return. Thomas had always thought of that song as nothing more than a childish tune. He had discarded religion long ago to master knowledge and pursue medical science. How could a highly trained doctor sing with sincerity words he had scorned his whole life? Would it not be hypocrisy? Still the joy of Elena made him long for what she had. He desperately wanted to sing her little song—to join her with hope in Jesus.

Chapter 5 - David

"So Samuel took the horn of oil and anointed him in the presence of his brothers, and from that day on the Spirit of the Lord came upon David in power." 1 Samuel 16:13

A Dark Battle

Elena was gone. The ache of not hearing her beautiful voice only intensified with time.

"What about me?" Thomas moaned. "Sweet Jesus, please, let me hear Elena sing just one more time."

Silence.

Wandering and calling out Elena's name, Thomas soon became hopelessly lost, and had to stop. Standing still, he strained to hear her voice, waiting for a clue as to which way to go.

Silence.

Time had no meaning, no sense of day or night; minutes felt like hours. Without sensation to orient his mind, he began to lose a sense of boundary between himself and the surroundings—*Am I anything at all?* With that question floating to the surface, a dreadful thought popped into his mind. *Am I slowly becoming part of the mist? Are little bits of me breaking off and being ab-sorbed into the grayness?* His mind began to ram-ble. *Well, at least being nothing, I will not have to worry about being swallowed by the black hole. But what if this grayness is endless? Condemning me to wander, going nowhere, waiting for nothing, meet-ing no one… alone.*

Thomas grew remorseful when he thought of all the times he had ignored people, and now he only wanted someone… anyone. *My life is nothing. I have pushed aside everyone: my wife, my daughter, friends. Even Elena has walked off and left me like I did to her at the orphanage. I have been a fool. For I've only cared about my achieve-ments in medicine… things with no value here. Why didn't I pay more attention to the people in my life?*

Thinking about the shallowness of his life only pulled Thomas further into despair. *Surely, there must be others like me lost in this fog. Should I search for someone, or wait? How long have I been standing here? Where is here?* His thoughts sudden-ly coalesced into a horrible question—*Will I get so lonely that I will choose to be swallowed by the black hole? Which would be worse, forever alone in this gray mist, or being tormented with others in the black hole?... Stop! I can't let myself think about this.*

Pulling himself together, he tried thinking of food. *I have had nothing to eat in a long time, but I don't feel hungry... and what about sleep. I'm not tired, yet I haven't slept in ages.* Cut off and alone, his mind drifted with the grayness. No night or day, no way to mark the notion of time... *Who can be sure of anything in the fog?* "What's happening to me?" Thomas talked out loud, wanting to hear a voice, any voice, even his own. "Someone, please... I need some answers... is this all there is... will the darkness be trying to get me?" His mind wrestled with reality. "Maybe the black hole has gone, or better yet, it was just my imagination... How do I know for sure?... You can't just let me live like this!... Am I forgotten?... Am I nothing?... is anyone there? SOMEONE, ANSWER ME!"

Silence.

Thomas struggled to discern between hallucinations and reality. He started to wonder if Joshua and Elena were real or just dreams. Life... existence in the gray mist held its own troubles—

a mind numbing tedium of endless gray with no variation.

"Let me see something, please… I can't live like this. Have pity on me!" he yelled.

Silence.

Frantic thoughts tugged at his sanity, but buried down deep, Thomas worried about the black hole coming to claim him. "Stop it!…" he screamed at himself. "Think about other things, not the darkness… I need light to live, not death." The volume of his rants increased, as if loudness would give the words authority to control the fear. "Don't let your mind think of the black hole. Stay calm. You can reason your way through this." Little by little, his grip on sanity slipped. "Is this grayness all there is? No, I must have hope like Elena. She made it through… Oh, what's the use." The more he yelled, the more his anxiety mounted. "What was the song Elena sang? Those words, what were they?" Thomas frantically searched for the memory, but to his dismay the song had slipped away into the mist. "Elena, come back, I want to hear your song."

"I'll just start walking." Thomas yanked himself from despair of not being able to remem-

ber Elena's song. "I am bound to run into someone… Wait, didn't Joshua warn me about taking
a wrong step and falling into a hidden pit?" The
debate with himself did nothing but heighten his
angst. "I can't just stand here waiting. What if
something worse were to come upon me?"

In desperation, he got down on all fours
and probed the grayness with his hand. After being assured of solid ground, he would slide a few
inches and probe again. Soon, his mind swelled
with dreadful images of what his hand might
come upon, like shoving your hand to the bottom of a muddy pool, wondering if something
lurks below. Nightmarish thoughts pummeled his
mind with dread of touching the unknown. Finally, the pain in his knees from kneeling on peb-
bles forced him to stand.

"Elena, Joshua, come back!" Thomas
yelled, again trying to hold on to some hope. "I
want to hear more. Show me which way to go to
the light." His shout did not even arouse an echo,
but died in the mist.

"Well, if something is going to happen,
let's get on with it," challenged Thomas. His attempt at bravado faltered on his lips, eclipsed by

the sound of his deepest fear—the sound of approaching evil. A low lurching rumble moved beyond his sight, triggering a flood of anxiety. "Think about medicine or how much you have accomplished in life." Unfortunately, these thoughts fell apart before the fear now arising. He heard the oozing off to the left. Then the acrid smell of sulfur wafted in, leaving no doubt of who waited for him. Stomach acid rolled up in his throat bringing along with it a nasty taste of vomit. He tried to swallow, but it stuck, making him gag. Thomas froze, hoping to hide in the stillness, but he knew the horrible thing wouldn't stop. Fear pulsed with each moment of waiting for death to appear.

Unable to constrain himself, he yelled, "Halt! You have no business with me."

Laughter shook the mist.

"Ah… show yourself or go back from where you came," Thomas cried out, tortured by not knowing what would come next.

Unearthly silence hung in the air.

To go from Elena's embrace—the eternal hope of glory, to being stalked by a black hole reeking of death… it drowned his mind in anxious remorse. To lose all hope and know the bliss of what you have lost, is far worse than being hopeless with no knowledge of what could have been. He felt his sanity wobble with panic and the thought of what now pursued him. He had tasted a little hell in experiencing Elena's life in the Sighetu Orphanage. The thought of unending darkness for all eternity brought with it waves of dread, yet being left in the grayness offered no relief either with its own insanity and loneliness.

"Doesn't my life deserve something better than this?" Thomas wailed.

From somewhere in the mist an ominous voice spoke. "You know what you deserve. You have put off this moment long enough; now it's time to join me, don't you agree? Few can hold out in this gray lonely wasteland, but you'll have plenty of company in me. It is where you belong—the end of all ends."

That last statement shook Thomas. "End? No, I need more of life, not an end to life." He dropped back and placed his hands on his knees wanting to throw up, but nothing would come up except a thick acid that burned.

Bubble, slurp, swish, the sounds grew closer.

"O God, no," cried Thomas. "Why was I even born if this is my end? Tossed into the dark pit like a piece of filth… swallowed by terror with no hope. Someone, please help me! Is there no justice for all I have done?"

"Oh Thomas, stop it, you're hurting my feelings," chuckled the voice. "If you put up a fight, I will let you stay in this gray mist until you go insane screaming gibberish, begging me to take you in… Well, honestly having you go a little crazy makes it more enjoyable for me. Once you are in here and get settled, you'll find the screams of others rather enjoyable too. I mean, there is not much else to do. You either feed upon their screams, or they will feed on yours. Once you get the hang of it, you will know how to prod others' distress to increase the feast."

"No," protested Thomas. "I want to go back to earth and choose what really counts, faith and hope."

"Oh, you want a 'do-over' because you met with Joshua and Elena and saw something better. Their words hold no power here. Your life has been spent pursuing other things; now you must pay the piper." The voice dripped with menacing sarcasm. "Such pleading for goodness will be of no help with me, or as they say back on earth, 'over my dead body.' Well, actually it's your dead body, but the meaning is the same—'to hell with you.'" The black hole began to laugh at its own little joke.

The acrid stench clawed its way into Thomas' nostrils and throat, making him gag over and over.

"I can't get my breath," choked Thomas.

"That's why they call it death," the dark hole guffawed, pumping out even more noxious fumes. "Now here is where you say, 'Stop it, you're killing me.' And then I say, 'That's the whole point.' Ha ha, my jokes are such killers." With each laugh, more of the sickening gas rolled over Thomas. "Really, do you think anyone cares about you?... Oh, that's right I do... but only as a meal." A chorus of profane laughter erupted from the hole.

In panic not knowing what else to do, Thomas gasped, "Lord, have mercy... Sweet Jesus save me!"

A Question of Love

A ball of puke formed in Thomas' throat. He wanted to gag it out, but it only became thicker and cut off his air. "I can't… can't breathe!" Panic flooded in with each wheeze, and darkness descended like a curtain over his sight. He fell to his knees with a crunch. "Help me…"

Suddenly, a trumpet blared somewhere far off, and the sound made the darkness stop its ingestion of Thomas.

Stomp stomp. Thomas heard someone marching toward him, pounding the gray stones with each step.

The evil shivered at the sound of approaching feet and lost its grip. Thomas wrenched himself away and collapsed into a quivering lump. The glob of spit dislodged in his throat, and he coughed it out, rejoicing with the flow of each new breath.

"Hey, buddy," came a warm, friendly voice. "It appears you're having a breathing problem. That nasty black hole can really make breathing tough." A quick slap on the back made Thomas cough up another plug of phlegm, and the obstruction in his lungs eased. Each breath now greater than the previous, slowly dissipating the stench of decay. He rubbed his eyes trying to clear the grime, for he wanted to see who had come to his rescue. Drenched in sweat, Thomas continued to gulp in air and worked to calm himself.

"Oh, Thomas, my friend, you had a close call with death I'd say."

Thomas nodded, breathing deeply. He wiped the puke from his nose and mouth. "Thank you for saving me," rasped Thomas. His voice was still recovering from the tight grasp of the black hole. "But I don't understand. Who are you? I was hoping for…"

"Joshua or Elena… I know, but I wanted to come."

"And you are?" asked Thomas.

"David, at your service," beamed David. He cleaned the grime from Thomas' eyes and helped him stand. David's smile sparkled with joy, putting Thomas immediately at ease.

Thomas looked at the glorious face of David and spoke. "Thank you for coming to my rescue. What do you call that thing that almost swallowed me?"

"Death," said David.

"But I thought I had already died to get here." Thomas said, still shaky from his ordeal.

"Oh, the first death on earth is merely a passing through to this place of desolation. The real death is what almost swallowed you," David replied.

Thomas breathed out long and slow, thinking about what had nearly happened. "How do I keep it away?" he asked. "It laughed at me like I was nothing but a bag of chips to feed upon." Even now the thought of that putrid odor made Thomas want to retch.

"You and I have no power over death," said David.

"But it left when you came. It obviously cannot tolerate your presence,"

"Not exactly. It cannot abide God's presence in me; of myself, I am nothing," with those words David's face sparkled with joyous laughter.

"Then don't let God leave!" pleaded Thomas. He coughed again, bringing up more dark phlegm.

"You can relax about that. I'm God's favorite—He will never leave me," David said without a hint of self-importance. "Here, let me give you some of heaven's freshness to soothe your breathing," David took a deep breath, puckered his lips, blew its purity toward Thomas.

The air became cool and sweet, like sucking on a wintergreen candy. The horror of what Thomas had just experienced faded, replaced by curiosity over this "favorite" of God.

David stood before Thomas dressed in a robe of brilliant undulating colors edged with gold and sparkling stars. His luminescent blond hair like a crown around a joyous face. He didn't look powerful in appearance like Joshua, or beautiful like Elena, instead there emanated a sense of royal delight that lifted you up with joyous favor. Thomas could hardly find words to describe the aura about David. It made Thomas feel like he was David's extra special friend. Thomas could not think of anything on earth that matched the honor of David choosing him to be his buddy."

This must be the prince of heaven, thought Thomas.

David put his arm around Thomas and laughed, "I am not the prince, but I am a child of the king and the apple of His eye." Then with a warm hug he added, "It is so good to see you again."

Thomas didn't have the vaguest idea what David meant by calling himself a child, for that did not fit with his majesty and stature. Thomas had a good idea why David would be dearly loved by God, for love poured out of David, making him a joy to be around. But as hard as he tried, he couldn't place where they had met before. Though that mattered little right now, because David had saved him from being choked by death. "I don't remember our previous meeting, but I am sure glad to meet you again," laughed Thomas.

"And I'm glad to be of service to you," David said with a smile that bathed Thomas in goodness, joy and love.

David's warm demeanor made Thomas relax, pushing aside his anxiety over the dark hole. Thomas marveled at the contrast of one moment being caught by eternal darkness, and the next being surrounded with light and life that radiated from David. It reminded him of the light he had first seen upon coming to this gray mist, only now with David, it did not burn or cause him to squint.

Who could he be?... I should know him. Thomas searched his memory, but came up blank.

"I understand if you don't remember me," said David, seeing puzzlement in Thomas. "But like Joshua and Elena, God used you in my life to make me what I am." He gave Thomas another big hug and joyful laugh. To answer your questions, we should start at the beginning of my life where the love of God first touched me.

"Wait," Thomas said, concerned about another experience like at the Sighetu orphanage. "What do I say if it is too painful on me? I mean, take a breather from…" Thomas felt a surge of shame that he had offended David by implying his life might be awful.

David looked at Thomas for a long time before speaking. "Love caused God to step in and take my pain. It is my hope it will teach you that His love is better than life, and life without the love of God is unbearable. For His love can transform even the most dreadful life into a blessing. Thus, love becomes the measure of life, not pain. If my life becomes too much for you, just pray— 'Oh, for the love of God.'"

David reached out his hand to Thomas.

"But…" Thomas protested but didn't get a chance to finish.

Whoosh.

First Breath

Thomas found himself bundled in blue cloth, staring up at fluorescent lights. Looking around, he could see nothing but white flannel walls. Just above his head hung a blue card with a pudgy infant angel holding a horn that blared out the words, "It's a boy." Under that, someone had handwritten D-A-V-I-D.

This must be David in his first few hours after birth, Thomas thought. *But why bring me to this beginning stage of life? How is this going to show me anything? He's just a newborn.*

As Thomas acclimated to the setting, he felt a great deal of anxiety and fear coming from David.

"Ammmmmph," David struggled and grunted with each breath, "ammmmmph." Working hard to get the next, "ammmmmph." Thomas felt a rising apprehension with David's struggle to breathe. *Something's wrong!*

"Over here doctor," said a female voice. "We are keeping him separate until you can examine him."

The face of the doctor appeared over the crib. It shocked Thomas to see a face that looked very familiar. It all came clear when he saw the name tag, Dr. Charles Bennet, Resident Physician, Deaconess Hospital. *It's my mentor during his training!*

"Nurse, unwrap him for my exam," ordered Dr. Bennet.

Thomas felt David being quickly unswathed. The cold air hit his body like a shock, "Waa…" David tried to cry but halted. That's when Thomas noticed David lacked the strength to sustain wailing. Immediately it turned to a whimper, "aaammmmmph," a silent struggle for

the next breath. David did not move or cry because air hunger necessitates complete concentra-
tion on the work of breathing. Underlying all this
is the fear of not being able to keep up. Each inhalation not full enough for comfort, followed by
panic-driven exhalation; fear fighting with exhaustion in each grunt.

I can't breathe, I can't breathe! bounded
through David. In the distance, Thomas heard an
ominous sound—a gurgling. *Is that David's
breathing, or something else?*

After Dr. Bennet finished his exam of
David, he went to the nurse's station to write in
the chart. The nurse, while re-wrapping David,
noted an ashen color and placed an oxygen mask
on him.

The soothing oxygen began to allow David
to relax.

Thank heaven for this nurse, thought
Thomas.

As the nurse held the oxygen mask around
David's nose and mouth, she whispered a prayer,
"Lord, help this little baby survive."

The fear and gurgling backed off. *Must be
the oxygen,* thought Thomas.

"Nurse what are you doing? I didn't order any oxygen," scolded Dr. Bennet looking up from his charting.

"But, this baby is struggling and turning blue. I just wanted to help him breathe."

"This is obviously a child with Down Syndrome and severe heart defects," He admonished the nurse. "I still have to talk to the Hansens to see if they want to do anything, but I think they will just want to let nature take its course. His quality of life will be marginal at best. He's hardly worth the trouble he'll put his parents through. It may be more humane to let him die now than to put him through extensive surgery only to endure a slow, excruciating death in some institution."

"Forgive me doctor. I only thought the oxygen would help until the parents decide," she volunteered.

"Since you have started the oxygen, leave it alone," rebuffed Dr. Bennet. "But remember, ethically, it is always easier to withhold treatment than to take it away. Don't do anything further until I return from informing the parents of their options."

After Dr. Bennet left, the nurse quickly prayed, "Lord, grant the parents wisdom in their decision... and be with David no matter what happens."

In a few minutes, Dr. Bennet returned looking flustered.

"They didn't even give me a chance to explain the problems this child will face," He complained to the nurse. "How can they claim God loves this baby when it's obvious he will never be normal, or do anything worthwhile?"

"Maybe they love him, and that is enough," offered the nurse.

"So now we'll expend a lot of effort, and waste a lot of money—Oh for the love of God, don't they see that if God really loved this child, He wouldn't have let his chromosomes get messed up in the first place." Dr. Bennet finished writing the orders calling for a transfer to Children's Hospital for further workup and possible heart surgery. Then he slammed the chart closed and threw it in the nurse's direction. "What kind of life is this kid going to have? I'll tell you what kind—a big fat expensive zero... religious fanatics," and stomped out of the room.

Tears formed in the nurse's eyes as she tucked David under his blanket and positioned the oxygen mask.

"Oh, for the mighty love of God," she prayed under her breath. "May God's love be with you all the days of your life, and may His love touch those around you... even Dr. Bennet."

Even Dr. Bennet? Thomas bounced between thoughts. *David has Down Syndrome! Dr. Bennet tried to give the best care as he saw it. How could he have foreseen that David would turn out so... so glorious?*

With the oxygen, David fell asleep and didn't awaken until being lifted into the arms of his mother.

Looking around, Thomas realized the transport crew had brought David to his parents for one last visit before being taken to Children's Hospital.

"Oh my darling David, you are so precious." David's mother smiled. With tears pouring down her cheeks, her love washed over David. "I want you to know we will be praying for you; no matter what the future holds. We trust the love of God to protect you and be a banner over your life for however many days He gives you." Then she started to kiss David, and anoint his head with her tears.

A man leaned over, kissed Betty, then whispered, "Darling, we have to let them take David now."

"Oh Jack, let me hold him just a little longer," pleaded Betty.

"We'll get the doctor to discharge you so we can drive over to Children's Hospital and be with our son."

"It is so hard to let him go. He's so small and fragile. What if something happens on the way?"

"It's just a few miles and they'll take good care of him," reassured Jack. "Besides, God loves him far more than we can imagine. I'm sure this is just the first of many times we'll have to trust in His love." Jack leaned over and kissed Betty. "I memorized a verse for David's birth. Little did I know how pertinent it would be to what we are going through, 'May the God of hope fill you with all joy and peace as you trust in him, so that you may overflow with hope by the power of the Holy Spirit.'"

"Thank you, I have to just keep reminding myself that our hope is in God." responded Betty.

Jack took David from Betty, gave him a kiss, then placed his hand upon David's head and prayed, "Lord, may your love abound to David and use his tiny life for your glory, Amen." He then handed him over to the transport nurse.

A cascade of love mysteriously splashed into every part of David and filled him with joy. David swelled with the goodness of life, and Thomas could only wonder at the miracle taking place before him. Though this disabled infant labored to breathe, love from his family and God put a different perspective on David's physical disabilities—his struggle to live became something to deepen their love. As ordinary parents, there were fears of what the future would bring and sorrow at what David would not be able to do. But bathed in love, all of it seemed mere obstacles they would scale together. The beauty of this moment swept Thomas up in joy. "Oh, for the love of God," slipped from Thomas's lips.

Whoosh.

"Brrrr," Thomas shook, jolted by the sudden return to dull gray emptiness. He quickly looked around and found David standing off to his left. "That parting with your parents, the intensity of… love," said Thomas. "I have never experienced it like that before. I wish it would go on forever."

"Oh, Thomas," smiled David. "Love is forever, for those who embrace His love and let it wash them clean."

Thomas then remembered Dr. Bennet, his professor and mentor, the one Thomas had looked to for guidance throughout his medical career. It was Dr. Bennet who had inspired Thomas. Even now, he could hear Dr. Bennet saying, "Perfection is what our patients expect of us, and nothing less will do." In fact it was because of Dr. Bennet's influence that Thomas specialized in genetics which led to all his groundbreaking discoveries.

"I hope you're not angry with Dr. Bennet," said Thomas glancing at David. "He's actually a very good man. He just didn't want you to suffer. Isn't that part of love too?"

"Love helps us endure suffering and can bring good from what seems a loss," responded David. "Love should be part of every..."

Thomas barely heard David; instead, he became caught up in his own thoughts of past discussions with parents about genetic errors and what it could mean for their pregnancy, offering the merciful option of termination. *Did I show love and compassion? I thought so...*

David answered the thoughts of Thomas, "My parents loved me for what God made me to be," said David. "Their love made my life worth-while."

"Wait, love can mean different things to different people," countered Thomas.

David sighed, "You followed the norms of society rather than the love of God. How can you show love when you don't know what true love is?"

Thomas became a little irritated, "I think an intelligent person can determine what is love for themselves."

"Love is not about knowledge," replied David. "On earth, everyone has their own idea of love, but until you experience the unconditional, enduring, sacrificial love of God,… well, you'll have no idea of the power of true love. Look at me, Thomas. I am the result of God's love, and I will continue to breathe deeper, more fully the deep and wide love that flows from heaven. That's what life is all about—learning to breathe the love of God."

With those words, the brilliance of David became blinding, causing Thomas to fall back. "Stop! It is too much for me," cried Thomas as he fell to the ground in shame. "You're hurting me!" Past words to patients about love played in Thomas' thoughts, "If you really love this child, then you would let nature take its course… Love won't sustain you through the arduous care of this baby's condition, it will just cause more suffering for you and this infant." Thomas cringed with each word he had uttered.

David broke in. "I see that you rightly re-member trying to use love as a tool to manipulate rather than a light to bring warmth and illumina-tion from God. The love you experienced at my birth is but a foretaste of what God wants to give to us… Love is the very air of heaven."

"No fair reading my thoughts," complained Thomas. "At least allow me to explain—we were trained in medicine to stay aloof and not become emotionally involved. The professors always expected us to maintain an objective / scientific point of view and never let our own personal beliefs enter the discussion. Decisions are hard enough without having to wade through all the emotion. Certainly, you can understand a doctor can't let love affect clinical decisions. You must remain neutral and rational, especially when it comes to genetics where it is a matter of probabilities. The parents can be caught up in an emotional frenzy, but the doctor must remain cool and analytical, concerned only with the medical facts.

"Is that all you think love is—just emotion?" said David. "Love brings forth emotion, but love supersedes it and sometimes works against emotion. Jesus in the days leading up to His crucifixion put aside his emotions and subjugated them to His love and desire to do the will of God. That act of love by Jesus showed the world true love."

Standing in the presence of David, where love shimmered in resplendence, Thomas felt shame in the shallowness of his ideas on love and life. But he had a point to make, an attempt to salvage some value for his life's work. "Why does God's love put some children through the agony of horrible defects? How is that love? On the flip side, aren't my accomplishments in ending these genetic errors a work of love?"

"The heart is deceitful above all things. You and Dr. Bennet portrayed your actions as compassionate, but they mostly originated in a strong sense of self-importance and intellectual pride."

Thomas started to protest, but then realized that his argument only added to the gulf between him and the love he witnessed in David. He began to wonder how he and Dr. Bennet had missed something so profound. *After all, they had been trained as doctors in the art of careful observation. How can you let love influence the difficult decisions of medicine?… I just don't see how it would work.*

"Your eyes still do not see. I am the result of God's love not the consequence of its absence." The light emanating from David grew in intensity so that Thomas had to shield himself with his arm.

"I want to see, but it is too bright, it blinds me," lamented Thomas.

David smiled, "Then let us go back to where it is more muted, so you can see and learn. I want you to witness a conversation between Dr. Bennet and the nurse concerning medical decisions about me. I think it will help you to see." He reached out and placed his hands on Thomas.

Whoosh.

Love Makes a Difference

Thomas found himself back at the hospital, but this time he floated above the scene observing Dr. Bennet writing in a chart at the nurse's station. Peering down with Thomas was David.

"Don't worry about Dr. Bennet, said David. "He can neither hear nor see us."

Dr. Bennet sat scribbling David's final discharge note. Muttering as if arguing with the chart before him, "What kind of craziness has this turned into? Do they really think they are helping this poor child?" he stopped talking when the door suddenly opened.

"Dr. Bennet, let me know when you are done and I'll make a quick copy of the medical notes for the parents to take with them to Children's Hospital," said the nurse.

"Here, take the chart," said Dr. Bennet. "As if it will make any difference."

The nurse raced out with the completed record to where Jack and Betty were anxiously waiting to be on their way. They longed to be with David and find out what could be done to help him at this critical stage.

The nurse wheeled Betty out to the car. Before helping her get in, she put her hand on Betty and prayed then pushed the wheelchair back to the OB ward. When she returned to the nurse's station, Dr. Bennet confronted her. "I saw you praying with the Hansens. You know there is a good chance the child won't survive heart surgery, and if he does survive, I don't think he'll live to see many birthdays. What kind of answer to prayer is that? Can't you see all this religious stuff is only going to make it harder in the long run?"

The nurse responded with indignation, "Can't you see they were just acting out of love for their baby?"

"Love! Where is love in all this?" countered Dr. Bennet. "It saddens me greatly to see a baby born with Down Syndrome, let alone having congenital heart problems. The life of an innocent child genetically messed up, parents grieving for what might have been. What kind of love allows that to happen?"

"I see it differently," said the nurse. "The love of God is not absent. It is God's great love that gives hope and the fullness of life, even in the darkest of times."

"Well, I don't see much love in it. I have seen too many tragedies, consoled too many grieving families to believe in the love of God."

"God's love is the measure, not what is measured," replied the nurse. "You don't see it because you're too busy judging by your own standards. Love is what gives life value, not the other way around."

"Why should we have to sacrifice so much of our limited resources on misplaced love?" fumed Dr. Bennet.

The nurse mustered all her courage, "Could it be that sacrifice is an essential part of love? Let me quote to you from a higher authority: 'In this is love, not that we loved God, but that he loved us and sent his Son to be the atoning sacrifice for our sins.'"

"Spare me the platitudes. I think I've had enough religion for one day," said Dr Bennet as he closed the chart and shoved it toward the nurse. Then he got up and left mumbling under his breath, "Oh, for the love of God."

Whoosh.

Blinding Pride

David stood quietly, letting the scene they had just witnessed sink in.

The gray mist swirled in silence as emotions tore Thomas in different directions. He had many times used his mentor's words about meaningful life as reasons for limiting medical care. Quality and quantity of life had always guided his decisions—what else is there? But now here, in David's presence, his career seemed rather hollow and shallow. Medical actions he had felt so sure about teetered ready to collapse, because they had been devoid of real love. Could he really have been that blind? Advice he once had pushed with authority now seemed like so much noise—tormenting more than helping. A great sadness rolled through Thomas. How could he hope for God's love when his life had ignored its importance? In this realm, all his accomplishments crumbled into a worthless heap of gray nothingness... they had no value without love.

Turning to David, Thomas finally broke the silence, "I don't know what to say. I just never realized what I had missed. What can I do to make up for what I have spent my life rejecting?"

"Nothing... All you can do is humbly throw yourself at the feet of Jesus and seek forgiveness. That is where we all must start," said David.

"But why would God forgive me now?" moaned Thomas

"It starts and ends with the love of God."

"Even when I don't deserve it?" asked Thomas. "I'd feel like such a hypocrite."

"That kind of pride is lethal," said David. "If you don't let go of your own self-condemnation and humble yourself seeking His mercy, you will end up trying to earn God's grace and love, which ultimately flies in the face of grace and leaves no room for love."

"Huh?" mumbled Thomas.

David continued, "God's love, rich and free, saved my life back then, and gives me life now. All by His doing, so I never have to worry about not deserving it or losing it. Here is the awesome part—none of it is me, all of it is because of Him! Who can turn that down?" David exploded with excitement.

"But your life had nothing going for it, that's why…"

"Oh, you misunderstand. I wasn't asking you a question… I was making a statement. The love my family shared with me made all the difference in my world. I just wish you could have seen it more fully; maybe then, you wouldn't have been so despairing for my life."

Thomas felt a pang of envy. *I wonder where life would have taken me if I had really experienced the love of God like David?* After thinking for a minute, Thomas got the nerve to ask David a question. "Do you think Dr. Bennet heard what the nurse tried to tell him about love?"

"What do you think? You knew him and worked with him."

"I don't recall him talking about love, and certainly not religion, but I know he cared for his patients—even you. He was a perfectionist though, and sometimes that striving for the ideal made him appear unloving. You can understand that, can't you?"

"Love is patient and kind," David smiled. "I hold no grudge against Dr. Bennet. There is no room for that with love."

Again Thomas paused to think. Finally, he haltingly asked, "Do you think Dr Bennet was a good doctor?"

"It is not my place to judge, but I think I know what you are really asking," said David. "You want to know if you were a good doctor?" Not giving Thomas a chance to answer, David went on, "You should know by now that good and love go hand in hand. So judge yourself, did you act in love?"

Thomas took a long breath to consider, "I mean, I know why Dr. Bennet said such harsh things about you and God. It's the strain of repeatedly having to make life and death choices. Sometimes those decisions don't work out and illness wins. You have to become callous, because becoming personally involved will tear you apart. You can't afford the luxury of love. You decide a medical course of action based on what offers the patient the best chance to survive and live a normal life. You can't allow love to muddy the waters of medicine. Like a soldier, sometimes you have to view people as things, or you just couldn't do your job."

"Without love, everything becomes a thing," replied David. "Life becomes survival of the fittest, with good being decided by whoever is still standing at the end of the day. Based on that value system, you, along with Dr. Bennet and the world, labeled me as no good. Not worth the expense of heart surgery. But in heaven, love is the air we breathe. The last are first, and the first gladly serve the last. Love makes life good, even my life with all its hardship. But those who do not love will be unable to breathe such richness."

"Forgive me," interjected Thomas. "I didn't mean for my sentiments to be taken personally. I am glad you had the surgery and lived. It's just that medicine has limited resources. Decisions must be made as to how they should be distributed for the ultimate good for society. If one person gets an expensive procedure or drug treatment, there may not be money left for others. So you have to ration out care, giving it to those who have the highest potential."

David just looked at Thomas and sighed, "You mean reserve limited resources for people with normal brains."

"No…" Thomas stumbled for words. "I mean obviously your life was… I mean is important. I'm just saying that medical reality forces us to use some method to judge a life. An assessment of a person's potential along with circumstances of their life may seem callous, but it's the best we've got. Obviously in your case, we were wrong to think of your life as worthless. You have to admit no one could have imagined you would turn out like…"

"Like this—reflecting the love of God." added David. "Don't you see? His love determines value, and it has nothing to do with one's abilities or circumstance."

The brilliance shining out from David grew more intense to the point Thomas had to shield his eyes. "Stop, it's too intense! I can't see!" hollered Thomas.

The light grew softer as David spoke. "Thomas, you've spent your life pursuing lesser things that have blinded you to what is the greatest gift—Jesus. In heaven we call that: 'no room in the inn' sin," David laughed.

"You're making a joke of my inability to see and understand," complained Thomas.

"Not at all. The sad truth is you are the one who made a joke of love and in so doing became lost to its reality. But enough of this philosophical talk. It will be easier for you to see through my eyes back on earth. We're just getting to the good part."

David reached out and put his hand on Thomas before another word could be said.

Whoosh.

Love's Touch

Thomas found himself looking out through David's eyes, swaddled and warm. A green oxygen mask covered David's face. Peering around, Thomas noted a sterile-looking hospital area enclosed in white curtains to maintain privacy. Jack rocked David swaddled in a warm blanket with Betty sitting beside them. Thomas guessed this to be pre-op at Children's Hospital. They must be awaiting David's heart surgery. Betty had placed one hand on David and the other she held raised up in worship. Normally, Thomas would dismiss such activity as worthless posturing of simple minds, more a diversion from worry than having any real chance for altering outcomes. But being in David, the recipient of Betty's prayer, he couldn't deny the love he felt pouring in from somewhere. This produced an aura of peace surrounding David that baffled Thomas. *How could such frumpy mumblings from Betty cause such a calm in David?*

"The surgical suite is almost ready for David," said the nurse, sticking her head between the curtains. "I'll be back in a minute to take him in."

Jack handed David to Betty and laid both hands upon David. One hand held the oxygen mask in place, with the other he took a little drop of oil and touched David's forehead. After a pause Jack took a deep breath and prayed, "We thank You Lord Almighty for David's life and ask You to protect him in the coming surgery. We know that the world looks at the outward appearance but that You look at the heart. As You anointed King David so many years ago, please now bless our David for the work of Your kingdom."

David's mother then spoke with tears running down her face, "David, my precious son, we have prayed for you every day since we knew you were coming. Though your father and I don't understand why you have to go through all this, we know God loves you and we love you. I want you to hear why we named you David, because you are a man after God's own heart, just like King David. Whatever happens in surgery, we trust that somehow your life will glorify God." Then Betty started singing, "Jesus loves you, this I know…"

David's spirit bubbled with joy at the song. *That's Elena's song that I couldn't remember.* Thomas rejoiced and cherished each word as the music brought back thoughts of Elena and her beautiful hope. *How could I have forgotten that song?*

"It's time," said a nurse, as she stepped into the room. "I will carry him into the operating room. You will have to go to the waiting room. Dr. Goddard, the surgeon, will come talk to you when it is over." She took David through a door that swung open and into a brightly lit green tiled operating suite.

As David lay on the operating table, the OR team made last-minute preparations, taping on monitors for heartbeat, temperature, and oxygen. Thomas knew what it all meant, but he could sense David's growing apprehension. That is when Thomas saw a warm glimmer begin to blot out the beeps and the clatter of the operating suite. The light brought soft music—"Jesus loves me, this I know…" accompanied by a reassuring sweet smell that supplanted the cold sterility of the OR. *Wow, whatever they are using for anesthesia is great stuff,* thought Thomas.

The calm continued to swell about David; even the OR staff appeared more relaxed. Thomas realized this tranquility didn't come because of the anesthesia, but because of something much more profound. It reminded him of the aura that had accompanied David when they first met in the gray mist. Thomas could not find words to describe the restfulness he experienced pulsating through David. Swathed in serenity, Thomas yearned to understand how this contentment came about. He wanted to have this peace in his own life. Ever so faintly, Thomas thought he heard giggling coming from deep within David. Searching for the source, he noticed it sounded like two people laughing with joy. He recognized one voice as David's laugh. The other laugh declared with power and pure delight in the joy of David's life. *Why, it is the Creator of all things taking great joy in David!* This revelation tumbled through Thomas, making him yearn to be part of God's happiness too. *Who would have guessed that the purpose of David is to give joy to God.* Thomas stretched to get his mind around something so mind-boggling.

Soon soft singing filled the life of David with wonders that Thomas could not fully grasp. As the song progressed, it knocked apart any notion Thomas had of David's little life being worthless.

A voice welled up in David that Thomas recognized as belonging to the light he had first seen in the gray land. "David, I will keep you as the apple of my eye and hide you in the shadow of my wings." The voice penetrated every part of David, causing a soft tingling. The Holy came upon David stirring a transformation from a defective infant into David—a dearly loved child of God. From the heart of heaven poured a soothing current of love. David breathed in this heavenly air, and with each breath the fear gave way to joy and peace.

How can this be? A baby with Down Syndrome undergoing heart surgery becomes the sole object of heaven's delight. Thomas never imagined that such a simple thing as love could make David's severe disability irrelevant, transforming David into a miracle of life by the deep affection of God. The eyes of Thomas's heart now witnessed something extraordinary—the Lord

Almighty kissed David, leaving His sublime im-
print upon this baby. Further words failed
Thomas. He could only think one basic truth—
Jesus loves David. So simple, yet beyond understanding, so wonderful it seemed preposterous.

"Oh, for the love of God," exclaimed
Thomas.

Whoosh.

Oh, For the Love of God

Back in the gray mist, David spoke first.

"Amazing isn't it," David could barely contain himself. "The Holy Spirit really knows how
to give peace in the midst of the storm."

"Yes, quite unbelievable," Thomas replied,
looking into the gray mist, trying to understand
what he had just witnessed. As he stared out into
the void, the joy and wonder faded, replaced by
questions and doubts. The gray mist had a sinister
way of dragging down life to look less miraculous
and more like a random coincidence. It desatu-
rated the color from memories, making them all
look gray.

"Use your common sense," popped into Thomas' mind with the scent of decay. The voice continued, "Don't get caught up with some emotional manipulation. Do you think love is going to help when a severely disabled life meets reality?"

"Thomas, don't listen to the voice of darkness; it's a lie," David warned. "The love of Jesus touched my life and made it full. Do I appear defective?"

The voice kept probing; "Come on now, your life of research in genetics did far more for the disabled than some trite saying like Jesus loves me. Real truth is only discovered by rigorous scientific application. You are too smart to be fooled by this religious jargon."

As the gray mist pummeled Thomas with doubts, he slipped into his old analytical mindset. Putting on his doctor's role, Thomas addressed David. "I am not sure how a few quaint words about love can make any difference in a baby who knows nothing, especially one with significant mental and physical deficiencies. I'm afraid life is more complex and difficult than that. Your simple mind was easily manipulated. Besides if God loves you why did he not heal you completely?"

David regarded Thomas with dismay over his blindness. "What is it going to take for you to see the truth? Open your eyes. Look at me, then look at yourself. Now tell me who has been healed, and who still needs healing."

Thomas wrestled with his lifelong conviction that the stories of Jesus were no more than myths, a wishful thinking of those who couldn't think for themselves. But standing here having met Joshua, Elena… and now David, his mind struggled. *But what about all the tragedies of life? How could the love of God be compatible with all that pain?*

David knew where Thomas struggled. He took a deep breath of heaven and spoke, trying to break through to Thomas. "Tragedy is not the bad things that happen in life. Tragedy is leaving the love of God out of what happens in life." David's eyes became moist. Something deeply moved him.

"You're crying?" Thomas said, looking at the tears running down David's cheeks.

"My tears are not from pain or sorrow, though I had plenty in my life. They are from gratitude for the love I received from Jesus and from my family, for it filled me to overflowing, giving me life in abundance, far outweighing any suffering."

Looking down, Thomas saw his gray limbs covered in open sores. *Is this what my life has come to?* Slowly he wondered if his understanding of life and what is a priority, might have been mistaken. "I do desire to have what you have," he said to David. "But I find naïve sayings like, 'Jesus loves me,' just too infantile."

"You didn't question the significance of these words with Elena," said David.

"Well, that's my point. She was nine, and I doubt she even knew what Becky sang to her. But, assuming she did know, it's obvious that her tortured life made her desperate, so anything would be a step up. Hope of any kind would help Elena to go on living," responded Thomas. "Love is a similar emotion that makes living seem better. But can love alter genetic defects?... Can love make what is useless into something useful?"

"It did in me," said David. "You are wrong because you do not know the promises of God nor understand His power."

"I'm wrong? Wait a minute, How could love do anything? You were a baby undergoing anesthesia. You had no rational thinking, no language… those words didn't hold any meaning for you. You're trying to tell me that a few words you could not understand can sweep in and change a damaged brain? You had surgery for the heart defect, but when you woke up, you still had Down Syndrome. Where is 'Jesus loves me' in that?"

"It is not some magical incantation to get what you want. That only drags love down to self-indulgence. Your intellectual skepticism completely ignores what God's love is doing. Jesus' love is the power of God at work to make me like Him. That kind of love is better than life."

Thomas shrank back and hid his eyes as again the light of heaven flooded through David.

David's voice grew loud, "You judge from the earthly realm of your five senses and hold God accountable to your own understanding. If something good happens on the spiritual level, you discount it calling it a psychological surge of emotion, and when something good happens in the physical realm you attribute that to medical skill as if the surgeon doesn't rely on God to heal where he has cut. There is no room in your heart for the love of God, because it is filled with yourself!"

David's last words hung in the air when a low rumbling shook the ground on which Thomas stood. Out of the mist a thunderous voice spoke, "Thomas, you think you are rich and need nothing, calling yourself wise by your own standards. But you do not realize that you are wretched, miserable, poor, blind and naked. You need to listen to Joshua, Elena, and David, for they are my humble servants with understanding refined by the trials of life. They can guide you to my forgiveness to cover your nakedness and give you My salve to put on your eyes, so you can see. But, be warned, you have little time left to discover true humility. My servant David, holds a special place, for he loves deeply. A love that overflows to those around him. David's smile warms the coldest heart, leaving no one outside. I have loved him since before he was born. I knit him together to be a special vessel of my love. When

he first cried out: 'I can't breathe — I can't
breathe, Lord, help me!' I answered his prayer—
'Look at Me, David, I am right here with you.
You can breathe in Me. I love you, and I want
you to be with Me forever. I have a special role
for you. You will be a man after My own heart,
just like King David whose name you bear.'"

> *A Psalm of King David*
> *"To you, O Lord, I called;*
> *to the Lord I cried for mercy:*
> *What gain is there in my destruction,*
> *in my going down into the pit?*
> *Will the dust praise you?*
> *Will it proclaim your faithfulness?*
> *Hear, O Lord, and be merciful to me;*
> *O Lord, be my help."*
> *Psalm 30:8-10*

"You have been named David which
means, 'dearly loved.' Though your life will be
hard and filled with many battles, I will be with
you. Let My love be the air you breathe."

> *You turned my wailing into dancing;*

you removed my sackcloth and clothed me with joy,
that my heart may sing to you and not be silent.
O Lord my God, I will give you thanks forever.
Psalm 30:11-12

When the thunder stopped, shame consumed Thomas as the words continued to echo in the air. Thomas turned to look at David and felt his skin burn with remorse for his ill spoken words on earth.

David looked at Thomas and said, "I dearly love God, but most important He dearly loves me. That is the air we breathe that gives life to life. What I received on the day of my heart surgery proved to be far superior to the defects in my life. It came about because of my parents' prayers and God's love for me and not my ability to understand or return love. Jesus gives to us when we don't even know what we need,… and what He gives to us is Himself. Jesus loves me. There is no greater power than that. All we need to do is receive it."

Thomas fell back as David's words made the air sparkle with joy. David took another deep breath, then exhaled goodness and love like light.

Thomas longed to breathe such air, but when he tried breathing in the light, it stuck in his throat, making him cough.

"Why can't I breathe the air you breathe?" rasped Thomas.

"Because you continue to see your experiences in life and medicine as somehow defining God's love. Instead, you need to let the love of Jesus define life's experience, even my Down Syndrome."

Thomas tried to take shallower breaths, but still it made him choke. Along with that it burned his eyes making him weep tears of regret.

"Come," said David. "Heaven desires to send you to a profound moment in your life where you chose the darkness over the light. But I won't be going with you, for it is your life, not mine." He reached out to put his hand on Thomas.

"Wait!" cried Thomas. "What words do I use to pull me out of my life and get back here with you? Don't misunderstand, I am eager to relive part of my life, it is just I…"

"To the contrary, I know that you have met death here in the gray lands. You are now fearful of the truth about your life and the choices you made," said David.

"That's not what I meant," said Thomas, trying to cover his fear. "I think I can handle my own life. It's just in case I want to talk to you about things... you know."

"You bet, buddy," laughed David. Then he proceeded to sing:

"My favorite words remain,
when all else will not sustain.
Oh, for the love of God,
becomes life's true refrain."

It irritated Thomas that David tried to make fun of his meager understanding of love with a poorly constructed poem. Thomas tried to protest. "Isn't that a little corny for..."

Too late, David's hand touched his shoulder.

"I will pray for salve to put on your eyes and humility to touch your soul," said David's distant voice.

Whoosh.

The Pain

Thomas found himself staring down on his younger self, scribbling into a patient chart, dressed in wrinkled green scrubs and a white lab coat. His hair pushed in different directions because of being pulled from sleep to the emergency room. His eyes showed signs of fatigue, and his hurried manner betrayed a desire to finish and crawl back in bed. A plastic badge hung from the chest pocket protector that read: Dr. Thomas Jones, intern. *I look exhausted,* Thomas thought, recalling the long hours of that first year in training. Looking around, he recognized the location——the Children's Hospital ER department.

A nurse walked up to the station and asked, "Any orders for your patient?"

"Yeah, get a CBC and UA…" said young Dr. Jones. "Oh, and send the kid over to radiology for a chest x-ray. With a fever and sore throat he may have a pneumonia." With those words, the horror of the unfolding tragedy came slamming back to Thomas. "STOP!" Thomas yelled at himself. "Think you fool, the boy's airway, and ability to breathe is about to shut down because of his swollen epiglottis. Don't let him leave the

ER. You must secure the airway!" Thomas became frantic attempting to make himself heard, but no one could hear his warning. The night continued to plod along in its fated rendezvous with death. The x-ray tech wheeled the three-year-old boy down the hall to radiology, all the while Thomas screamed attempting to catch someone's attention. Looking back at the ER nurse's station, he saw the younger Dr. Jones lay his head down on the counter to grab a few minutes of sleep. *Nooo...* The self-loathing and culpability from this night would plague him for the rest of his life. Now he watched, helpless to stop it. Thomas had kept this memory walled off in a corner of his brain for every time it resurfaced, terrible anxiety would drown him in fear and guilt, making it hard to breathe... hard to live. *God, is this punishment for my horrid error?* He wanted to run away and hide. *What were the words to get me out of this and return to the gray mist? O for God... something...* his mind couldn't think of anything other than the disastrous mistake about to happen. *I should have died, not this kid... Is this hell— reliving my shame?*

In the x-ray department the technician helped the boy onto the table and gave his mother a towel to wipe the saliva drooling from the boy's mouth.

"Something is not right," quipped the mother to the tech, "my son is having problems breathing."

"Then let's quickly shoot the chest x-ray and return to the ER," said the tech. "Help me to lay him down on the table, then step behind the door while I shoot the x-ray."

When the boy laid down for the x-ray, he began to cough and gasp followed by a sickening gurgle.

"Hold still while I take your picture; it won't hurt at all," The tech said as he scooted behind the lead-lined wall and shot the x-ray.

Suddenly, the boy started to choke… then he gagged and stopped breathing. Noticing the child's distress, the tech ran over to the youngster, rolled him on his side and slapped him on his back seeking to get him to take a breath; instead, the child went limp and turned blue. The tech hit the emergency call button and scooped up the boy and started running back to the ER with the hysterical parents scurrying behind, calling for help.

"Code blue radiology. Code blue radiology." Sounded overhead as Dr. Jones broke out of his lethargy, jumped up, and raced to the radiology department. He met the x-ray tech running toward the ER carrying the limp boy in his arms. The shock of the toddler's ashen face and thick bloody saliva dripping down his cheek made Dr. Jones sick with fear. Moving quickly back to the ER, a team of nurses and doctors converged frantically working to resuscitate the child. Sucking the mucus from the mouth and throat revealed the problem—a swollen red epiglottis had completely obstructed the child's airway. Multiple attempts at intubation to get a breathing tube around the epiglottis failed.

"Someone get the surgeon! He needs an emergency tracheostomy," the chief resident yelled above the turmoil.

Dr. Jones, panic-stricken, looked for signs of improvement, knowing he had missed the diagnosis and should have never sent this boy to radiology.

God help this child, don't let him die, spare him, please spare him! Dr. Jones prayed silently as he tried to push oxygen past the obstruction with a bag and mask.

"You're only pushing air into his stomach," the chief resident yelled at Thomas. "Get a 14 gauge IV. We can try punching it through the cricothyroid cartilage."

The ever slowing beep of the heart monitor thundered above the din of doctors and nurses struggling to save the boy. Thomas floated at the edge of the scene, his gut in a knot as he relived the worst night of his life.

"Why are you dragging me through this?" Thomas yelled out in anguish. "Does heaven wish to rub my face in my guilt and shame for causing this boy's death?"

The prayer of the young Dr. Jones seared through his mind. *God, don't you love this child? Do something! Save this boy.* Tears mixed with sweat dripped from Dr. Jones' nose. Suddenly, the heart monitor flatlined and let out a monotone buzz. With it, a young life slipped away.

The effort to resuscitate continued, but everyone knew the outcome, they were all grappling with their own sorrow. Finally, the Chief Resident said, "I am calling off the code. Time of death, 2:13."

Dr. Jones swore under his breath, "God, why did You let this happen?" Taking a little carved lamb from his lab coat pocket, he threw it across the room. The impact on the far wall broke off one of its legs. "Oh, for the love of God. I wish I had never been born."

Whoosh.

Thomas found himself back in the gray mist. The heartache and shame long buried now hit Thomas anew with full force. Looking up at David, Thomas started to cry, "Where was God's love?… How can you blame me for doubting? I prayed hard for that little boy, and God did nothing. God didn't help that child, and He didn't help me."

David came close to Thomas, put his arm around his shoulder, and the two wept together.

Off in the mist, Thomas heard a gurgling and noticed a whiff of sulfur. A reminder of his failure… of what he deserved.

After a long while Thomas asked David, "How am I supposed to learn about the love of God by reliving that terrible calmity? I had nightmares and bouts of depression for years after that night. It almost drove me out of medicine. Instead, I used it to push myself."

"You ran from your mistake then, and you are still running now." said David. "Life is filled with tragedy, but those times only become truly tragic when we refuse to run to God… to let Him bear our shame and failure."

"The kid died! How could it be more tragic than that? I wish it would have been me dying, not that innocent child."

"And you still carry the guilt," added David.

"I could barely live with myself, if not for Dr. Bennet counseling me and pointing me into genetics. I don't know what I would have done. He saved me, not God."

"Oh, but the nightmare is more hopeless if you blame God or even worse treat Him as a myth, for then you cut yourself off from God's mercy and love. What you truly need is forgiveness and hope that God will use the tragedy for good. If God can mold my life, which Dr. Bennet labeled worthless, into something good, then He can do the same for you. It is a wonderful part of God's love that through Jesus all out failures are redeemed as well."

"Wait a minute. There were many ways God could have prevented that child from dying, but He didn't. How can anyone believe in God or His love after that?"

"If you never learned to trust in the love of Jesus for the little problems of life, then it's difficult to trust in His grace and love for the big tragedies."

"You're dodging the issue. God let that boy die. Where's the love in that?"

"No, God's love let Jesus die, so we might live. That love you have seen in Elena, Joshua and me is what brought us through life's dark valleys. He anoints us with so much more in Jesus that we wouldn't have wanted life to be any other way."

David stood, his face beaming with joy and reflecting heaven's brilliance. Thomas had to cover his eyes but pressed on with his grievance. "I have heard that excuse for God's failure to help so many times…'you just need to have more faith' they say. Well, it's all a bunch of hogwash and doesn't work for me. I find it too foolish to be of much value."

"You mean God didn't answer your prayer the way you thought He should. You don't want to trust God, because He didn't live up to your idea of love," responded David. "Your guilt and grief over this boy's death grew into anger toward God. Spurning Jesus, you turned your back on God and walked away from His love."

"No," objected Thomas. "I didn't walk away, God did. I carried that heartache my entire life. I let it push me to even greater heights of achievement."

"Oh, Thomas," said David. "Your heart became hard to wall off the pain of that child's death. You made medical achievements your god, hoping to atone for that moment. By not seeking God's mercy, you missed out on God's love altogether."

"And what did you expect me to do?" said Thomas, barely maintaining his composure. "Tip my hat and say thank you?"

"Your anger has made you blind and deaf to the love of God. Can't you see? You judged God's love to be deficient and rejected it. You put yourself above God, holding your guilt above His mercy and grace."

Thomas grew sullen at the memory of that little boy. *If only I had not been so tired, I might have picked up on his airway difficulty.* The words 'if only' kept slicing at his heart. It took every ounce of effort he had not to run away into the darkness to hide, and he would have, if not for David grabbing and holding him in his moment of horrible shame.

Thomas began to cry, heaving with great sobs.

"You took up anger toward God from your anger toward yourself. Don't you see? Anger consumed your whole life. It pushed you to achieve in an effort to pay for your failures," said David. "To be honest, no amount of achievement can offset our mistakes."

Thomas tried to pull away, but David would not let go.

After a few moments David continued, "God's love is the ultimate measure of life. Without it, life is deficient. The error you made is demanding that God fits into what you think God should be, thus you blinded yourself to the powerful love God has sent in Jesus."

"Are you saying that God's love was there, and I missed it?"

"By the power of God's love, my life is not a tragic mistake as deemed by Dr. Bennet and you. I am David, dearly loved by God. We should pray and ask God to open your eyes so you might see the truth," encouraged David.

"Wait, I know my error, and I can't just discount it by throwing around some cliché about God's love. Honestly, a part of me died with that child. I don't think a prayer after the fact will make much difference for my grievous mistake or for the loss to that family."

"No, Thomas, you don't know. Your fatal error is underestimating God's power, nor do you comprehend the greatness of His love for us in Jesus."

"Power to do what?" Thomas struggled to stay in control of his emotions. "Go back and change my horrible mistake?"

"Better than that, Jesus gives life where there is death. He takes our hurts, mistakes, and sins and gives us His life."

"I can only wish it were true, but I have carried this for so long, it has become part of me." Thomas felt tears running down his face and turned away from David, trying to hide his lack of composure.

David gently spoke, "You're struggling with whether to let go of your shame and believe that God has the power to redeem something that happened long ago or continue to hold on to it… I think the best choice is obvious, let it go."

"But it's so hard… I can't…" choked Thomas.

David looked up and prayed, "Jesus, I know you can make the blind see. Please heal Thomas that he might see Your power and glorify Your name. In Your great love and mercy, open his eyes and ears and heart. Help him get beyond his own shame to hear, see, and know Your love. Let him see what You see."

Thomas felt David's hand rest on his shoulder.

Whoosh.

A Picture of Love

"David, are you ready to begin your birthday celebration?" said Betty.

David stood before a decorated table and took in the beaming faces of his family: his parents Jack and Betty, standing next to them, his brother Jerry and his wife Jan who held Samantha, David's one-year-old niece.

Betty, bubbling with delight, brought in the birthday cake. David's eyes jumped to each person in a kaleidoscope of joyous love. It surprised Thomas that David could see, as well as feel, love move about the room. David lacked the ability to read or communicate easily; instead, he saw with eyes that beheld more than the usual spectrum of light. A powerful surge of golden brilliance swept over everyone, and David could not contain his joy, so he began to sing, "Ahhhhhh Yooooo haaaa…" In this moment of jubilation, Thomas experienced a love in David that dwarfed anything he had known before. He could even understand the simple song rolling through David, though no one else could.

I love them, and Jesus loves me.
Jesus loves them, and so we see
The miracle of love encircling Thee.

"Let's all sit down, and we'll light the candles on David's birthday cake," suggested Jack. "Jerry, would you help your brother put on his party hat while I get the matches?"

"I'd love to," said Jerry as he grabbed two hats. "Come on, little brother, we'll go to the hall mirror to see how we look."

There before the mirror Jerry put on David's hat then his own.

"Marvelous," said Jerry.

"Yaaaa, yaaaa," cheered David.

Thomas saw in the reflection an aura of love and joy glowing about David and Jerry.

Jerry stood 18 inches taller than David, with brown hair and a big smile. David had blond hair cut short for easy care. He had thick glass that would only stay up on his nose if held by a strap. Even then half the time, they perched just above his nostrils. Constantly shoving up his glasses with his fingers left them smudged to the point of opacity. His eyes seemed to be in a perpetual happy squint. A round face atop round shoulders with no neck to speak of, a round belly with short stubby limbs and fingers, but he had the same smile as his brother.

Thomas couldn't help but see the radiance of heaven in these two. He envied them for this moment and truly desired to be part of the love they shared.

"Hey, you two, get back here so we can start the party," called Jack.

They all sat down. Betty lit the twelve candles and David took a big breath and blew out half of them. With the second breath, he got all but one. Finally, on the third puff, he succeeded. Everyone cheered and clapped, and Thomas did too, for breathing in the love in this family felt so good.

Jack and Betty handed David a present wrapped in fancy birthday paper with a big red bow.

"Orr mi?" voiced David with feigned surprise that only increased the laughter.

"Yes, David for you," said Jack. "As if you didn't know, funny guy."

David smiled and ripped open the package. Inside, he found a leather-bound Bible.

"David, look inside," urged his mother. "There are pictures."

"Oooo, yaa," David said as he turned the pages, for he loved the illustrations.

"See here is a depiction of David defeating Goliath. That is who you are named after, King David." said Betty as she gave her son a quick hug.

"Ahhhaaa," responded David.

He flipped through the Bible, looking at the other pictures. One that David held up for everyone to see showed Jesus, the Good Shepherd and drawn on Jesus' chest a large red heart with rays beaming down on the sheep. Thomas thought the drawing a bit cartoonish and trite, but David's whole being shouted pure joy as he gazed upon it.

David pointed to the heart drawn upon Jesus, then to his own chest. "Aaarrrt." Pointing his finger at the sheep in the scene, he uttered

"Eeeep." Moving his finger again to himself, David smiled and said, "Baaa baaa."

No one quite understood, but they all nodded in agreement.

Thomas experienced a wonderful love in David like nothing he had ever known before.

"Yes, David, you are My special lamb," came a voice from deep within.

David's happiness took off as he felt himself being hugged by his parents. For Thomas, this experience of love went far beyond anything he could describe. In fact, words would only distract from the love flowing at this birthday party.

"Look in front of the Bible," Betty's excitement broke into Thomas's thoughts. "Turn to the front page David. Your father and I signed it. Let me read it to you. 'To David on his 12th birthday. May you be a man after God's own heart. Always remember we love you, and Jesus loves you even more.'"

Below, David's mother had kissed the page with bright red lipstick.

David touched the page, tracing his fingers over the lipstick, then turned and touched his mother's lips. "ove yu," he paused, "Jes ove yu too," and he returned his parent's hug.

David glowed from being the center of attention. Thomas quickly looked at the cake, "Happy Birthday David," it said in blue swirls on white frosting. Thomas marveled at the joy filling the room. Through David, he could feel it as well as see it, like an aura about each person coalescing into a blazing ball of thanksgiving for life. With everyone smiling, laughing, and sharing the goodness of each other, this was a birthday celebration no one could have imagined twelve years ago. Above it all, Thomas sensed heaven joining in jubilation.

"Ya-ya-ya," said David, pointing at the cake. "Burday caa." He got up and gave his mom and dad another hug and patted them on the back. "Awww yu,"

Betty proceeded to cut the cake, giving David the first slice. Thick white frosting with ornate flowers on lemon cake, just the way David liked it, served on his birthday plate, with a Pepsi Cola in the special birthday glass. David actually preferred his Pepsi out of the bottle, but not on this day, for that didn't fit his image of a birthday celebration.

In that moment, Thomas discovered David thought in pictures, not words. He measured everything by an internal vision of what it should be. Thus, this day fit the birthday image, and therefore, he felt safe and comfortable. Where someone else might get bored with the same thing over and over, David needed sameness to fit the portrayal he had of every situation. Unexpected disruptions in the schedule caused the picture to not be right, which generated fear and anxiety. David's parents learned they had to prepare him for change by describing what would be different long beforehand so he could imagine a good picture of what to expect when change came. Along with the variance, they surrounded him with extra love for reassurance.

When everyone had a piece of cake, they lifted their glasses together for a toast from Jack, "Let us give thanks to the Lord, for He is good and His love endures forever, and we thank the Lord for David whose life has filled us with love."

Amazing. Thomas saw heaven's glory fill the room in brilliant luminescence, to the point he had to pull back, but David drank it all in. The others didn't seem to notice, except for Sam, who squealed with delight.

After finishing the cake, David got up and went around to everyone at the table, giving each a hug and telling them, "Jes ove yu." He saved the last hug for his parents. Standing between them, he pulled them toward himself and said, "ove yu." Tears streamed down their faces and filled the room with the fragrance of heaven. Joy and peace danced in the air and each breath begged for more.

The party came to a close, and Thomas felt a tinge of melancholy in David as Jerry got his family together to leave.

"Noooo…" cried David. He didn't want this day to end, and his sadness grew as they put on their coats to go. He gave his baby niece, Sam, one last hug and watched Jack and Betty give out parting kisses. They waved good bye out the front door, then it closed.

"Don't be sad," Jack comforted Betty. "We'll see them again at Christmas."

"It is just Sam is growing so fast and soon will be walking and talking. Before we know it, she'll be going to school…"

"Whoa, one day at a time," interjected Jack. "You can make a special trip to see them if you like, but I won't be able to go as I have no vacation left this year. Besides, someone needs to stay home to watch David." Jack gave Betty a hug. "Now let's get this house picked up."

David watched from the window long after Jerry's car had disappeared from view. Some words his father had said kept repeating in David's head—*someone needs to stay home to watch David. The sadness of his father and mother must be from having to care for him.* David's eyes filled with tears. The ability to read other people's feelings was a blessing in times of joy, but a curse when dealing with sadness and sorrow, for David could only guess as to the reason and sometimes he guessed wrong.

Thomas noticed a battle going on in David. On one side stood the love of His family and God. On the other side clamored the malevolent forces of darkness spewing out lies. *Jerry is a real son, not you. He can have a family and his own house. You can't even talk right. You are not worth anything.* These words weren't fully understood by David, but their despondent aura crushed every happy thought. A dark shadow of shame and self-loathing came over David. *You'll never be a real man. What girl would ever love you? Your mom only says she loves you, but underneath you hurt her by your existence—you can't do anything for yourself. You just make more work for everyone. Your father can't go see Samantha because someone has to babysit you. It would be better if you had never been born. Face it, you are just one big mistake. Your brain is no good, you're ugly, and you're a burden. You should have died at birth. God rues the day you came into being.* David pictured in his mind standing with his brother looking in the mirror admiring their birthday hats. To David's horror, his hat and face melted into a grotesque mess. His mind gasped for air as it choked with despair.

"God! lamented Thomas, Why are You allowing this? Didn't you just say David was special in Your sight? How can you let evil torment this boy and not do something? How does this show the love of God? It's not fair; he can't defend himself. His mind isn't capable of refuting these lies."

The scene in David's mind shifted to his family sitting at the table laughing, not for the joy of his birthday, but laughing at his empty chair. Soon this scene faded, replaced by voices, one of them Thomas recognized as Dr. Bennet, *"I didn't order oxygen, why did you give it to him?"*

"I just wanted to help him breathe," pleaded a woman's voice.

"Let nature take its course. His quality of life will be marginal at best, hardly worth the air he breathes."

It surprised Thomas that David held these memories from his birth. David had formed emotional impressions from what people said throughout his life, the more hurtful, the deeper the impression. And now the darkness manipulated them to tear David apart, destroying any love or joy he might have.

David's breathing tightened with the steady drumbeat of Dr. Bennet's words repeated over and over, *"not worth the air he breathes… better to have never been born."* Self-disgust grew, constricting David's throat, causing his fear and sadness to build. The attack from the darkness continued with the dredging up of past scenes of ugliness, hurt, and shame in David's life. A constant attack upon David coating everything with ugliness.

Thomas realized that David's mental capabilities weren't that deficient, just different. One of his biggest problems lay in a lack of verbal skills for communicating. To make up for this, he relied on sounds, vocal tones and pictures to understand and communicate. Often, David carried around magazines and used the photos to get his point across. Numbers and abstract concepts were not easily formed into mental images and therefore, difficult for David to comprehend. But he had a highly skilled ability to read people's emotions. He did this through a heightened awareness, subtle hints of voice inflection and body language. He could literally feel what others were feeling. These impressions became colors that David attached to events in life, along with a picture of the people involved. Thomas now understood that David's happiness on his birthday came not from presents or cake, but from seeing and feeling the joy of those celebrating with him. His goal in life consisted of seeking joy, love and peace for those around him. Seeing these attributes blossom in others blessed David too. Unfortunately, this amazing sensitivity came with a downside; he had an increased susceptibility to negative emotions. The sadness in his parents, when Jerry and his family drove away, he readily picked up, but here the darkness played a trick on David. By injecting the negative tone from Dr. Bennet about his life not being worthwhile, David wondered if his parent's sadness was due to his disability—not being able to measure up to his older brother. He would never be normal like Jerry and have a family to love. These sullen thoughts attached themselves to David's recent picture of standing next to Jerry in front of the hall mirror.

A war raged in David, with ugly scenes trying to ruin any joy David might remember from his birthday party. Unfortunately, David lacked any defense against these vicious attacks. His mind, unable to counter with reason, crumbled under the weight of repulsive images about himself. He sank before the noxious fumes emanating from the dark hole. From the billows of sulfur a moaning specter arose, whispering with David's voice: *"Mom and Dad are sad because they want*

Jerry's family to stay, instead they are stuck with a dummy."

This disgusting lie cast a shadow over every mental image David had of the family, producing further self-loathing and blame. *I should have died instead of living. The doctor said so.*

The picture of family began to change in David's thoughts, portraying him small, squat, and naked, standing apart from the family with his face distorted and blurred.

Who wants a worthless someone like me? Mom and Dad want Jerry and Sam to stay, not some dimwit. These thoughts and pictures bounced around in David's mind. *I'll never be smart like Jerry. I'll never have babies like Samantha. I am always going to be a burden, not a son. Stupid, stupid, stupid, that's what I am.*

Every few seconds the black hole would belch out noxious fumes and blow them toward David, expanding the darkness and making it hard to breathe. *My life is one big mistake. I would be better off having never been born—that's what everyone thinks, even Mom and Dad.*

It appeared to Thomas that hell sought to hurt David by using the feelings of sadness he sensed in his parents and twisting it into a lie that they felt bad about having David. A self-loathing came from the black hole as it tried to draw in its prey. Another picture popped up from the birth-day party—David and Jerry again standing in front of the mirror. In this image David looked small and ugly, his party hat morphed into a dunce cap. Jerry mocked and laughed at David using vile epithets. The putrid smell kept building until everything focused on ugliness in life. Like when kids at school had called him names, such as *retard… stupid…* the grotesque dunce cap inched down David's face… *moron… pin head,* pummeled his thoughts, *my brain is worthless, and my body is too… I should have died at birth like Dr. Bennet said.* Thomas could see the black hole trying to trick David.

"It's a lie, don't listen to it!" He cried out. But to no avail, Thomas could only observe and feel the heartache of David.

God, if You love David, how could You let the black hole do this to David? A sudden horror occurred to Thomas—evil was just reminding David of unloving words and feelings directed at him by people in David's life. Some came from classmates, some from the stranger's stares and whispers, and unfortunately some were Dr Bennet's.

"Awwwwww, me aawfllll," David cried aloud.

Betty walked over and put her arms around David. She knew something bothered him deeply because of the inflection in his cry.

"He's just sad that the party is over," said Jack. "He'll be okay."

"No, I think it is something deeper than that," Betty said, holding David close. Looking into his eyes, she asked, "What's wrong David? Do you hurt somewhere?"

"Eeeeeh," David pointed to his chest.

"Maybe he's sad that he can't hold Sam; you know how much he loves being an uncle," Jack offered. "I wish he could tell us what is upsetting him. It would sure make life easier."

"Well, he can't," said Betty defensively.

David looked at his father, then used his arm to cover his eyes as tears streamed down.

Can't... can't... can't, NO good brain, echoed through David.

David sat down on the sofa and cried into his hands. Betty sat down next to him put her arms around him, and sang one of David's favorite songs, "Jesus loves me this I know…" The familiar notes lifted his feelings and soothed the anxiety troubling David. Surprising Thomas, the music even quieted his own anxious thoughts.

The battle raged on with another belch of fumes coming from the darkness. *Hogwash, that's just a dumb little children's song. Your mom sings it to you because you are nothing but a stupid baby.* A photograph of the family formed in David's mind. In it, David had blurred to the point of disappearing. Another ugly whiff of decay blew in, coating everything with shame and sorrow.

"Naaa gggd, Naaw gggd" David's tears made it impossible to understand.

As the rotten odor continued to infiltrate David, his panic rose, *I can't breathe, I can't breathe!* A painful self-recrimination followed. *I am not worth anything. I can't do anything. No one wants me. I should never have been born… I'm sorry Mom and Dad for not being like Jerry. I know it hurts both of you; it hurts me too. I try, but I can't do much; I am such a useless disappointment.*

"… For the Bible tells me so. Little ones to Him belong they are weak but…" Betty had to stop being caught up in her own emotions… "He is strong." Betty finished by hugging David and praying over him. "Lord, show David how much we love him, even more how much You love him."

Pathetic, childish song, darkness mocked. *You're nothing but a useless baby.* The acrid fumes continued to smother David's thoughts. *You're all messed up; you even have to wear diapers like a little baby. Who are you kidding? Your parents consider you a burden and a disappointment, You'll never be a star football player like your dad, sing beautiful songs like your mother, or be smart like Jerry. You are a mistake.* The sulfur fumes continued to suffocate David. *Just think what should have been instead of what you are. Curse God for doing this to you… tell him you'd rather be dead!*

"Ahhhh." David felt weak and started to shake, his breathing became shallow and labored.

"Jack, something's wrong with David." Betty said, looking up to Jack. "He is not joining in on his song."

"Here, read to him from his new Bible. I have something I made for him that might bring some cheer." Jack handed her David's Bible. "I'll be right back; it's in the wood shop."

"Now where should I read from… I know, I'll read from the verses that have a drawing you'll like." Betty opened the Bible and began flipping through the pages, looking for just the right scene. "Aha, this is a good one." And she showed David a picture of Jesus standing in the midst of sheep, holding a little lamb in his arms.

Betty read, "I am the good shepherd; I know my sheep and my sheep know me—just as the Father knows me and I know the Father—and I lay down my life for the sheep." She finished reading and let David gaze at the illustration.

"We are all sheep and Jesus is our shepherd. We know He loves us deeply because He died for us. We just need to listen to his voice and follow him. You are like this little lamb that Jesus is carrying. That is why we named you David, because you are very special to God and to us."

Jack returned holding something wrapped in a white handkerchief.

"I didn't have time to gift wrap it, but I think now is the time to give it to you," Jack said giving it to David.

David stared at the lump in his hand for a moment. Another birthday gift yanked him from the awful thoughts that haunted him.

"King David started out as a shepherd, and God took him from that lowly beginning to be the King of Israel. I know Jesus has special things in store for you, so I carved you this as a reminder of God's love."

David unfolded the handkerchief to reveal a little wooden lamb.

Shock rolled through Thomas… *That's my lamb!… That's where I met David. He's the boy Carl beat up instead of me. He gave me the lamb.* Shame welled up in Thomas as he ruminated over the events of that day—Carl the bully, the bloody nose, his own cowardice. *That day turned the course of my life.* Thomas stared at the lamb and asked himself the question that he had asked every day since, *Have I made up for my cowardice?*

Thomas couldn't get away from the scene of the special-ed boy with blood dripping from his nose. His feelings of anger and humiliation came upon him afresh, and now knowing the story behind the lamb, Thomas felt even more guilt.

Jack's voice jerked Thomas from his thoughts. "Every time you look at his lamb, I want it to remind you of our love for you and God's love for you," As Jack said this, he gave his son a hug and holding back his tears said, "We love you David, but Jesus loves you even more than we do, and He has special plans for you in His kingdom."

David's picture of Jerry and him before the mirror slowly changed to showing two kings standing arm in arm.

"I ov yuuu," cried David as he embraced his parents. "Jeees ov mee."

The air became fresh and clear, each breath filled with love.

But why did David give me the lamb that was a present from his father? Thomas wondered.

For a long time Betty and Jack sat holding David in a warm embrace to emphasize how much they loved him. When Betty sensed David understood, she gave him a kiss and said, "Time for bed birthday boy. Go get into your pajamas and I'll send up Dad to say goodnight and pray with you."

Later as David laid in bed, he looked at the ceiling filled with the glow cast from the night-light. He began to softly sing.

"Jeees ov mee… Mum ov mee… Da ov mee… an I ov yuuu," and David fell asleep.

Thomas laid there too, thinking of all that had happened. *I have to tell David how sorry I am for all he endured from Carl and his gang. I should have stood up to them. Though when David hears how I used that simple lamb to spur me on to great medical discoveries in genetics, he'll see and feel good about the role he played. That must be why David met me in the gray mist, so I could tell him how much his gift meant to the world. I think I've learned that even the most disabled can be worth something. I think I'm ready now to walk in heaven's light. Now, what did David tell me to say to take me back to the gray mist? Oh, yeah—"O for the love of God."*

Whoosh.

Chapter 6 - The Last Gasp

"This is what the Sovereign Lord says to these bones: I will make breath enter you, and you will come to life." Ezekiel 37:5

Alluring Darkness

The grayness seemed thicker… heavier than before. Looking about, Thomas could not even see the ground or his feet. The disorientation of the heavy mist made him sink down and sit rather than risk falling. "David, I understand it all now," Thomas shouted out into the gray mist. "I am here to inform you of the great story of your lamb. How much of a difference your gift made in the world."

Silence

"David this is important. You need to hear this. It's why you were sent to me so I could tell you."

Silence

A soft female voice drifted out of the mist, "David got fed up with you and left. But I want to hear it, even if heaven doesn't care."

Thomas turned about, looking for the source, then froze when he smelled a slight whiff of sulfur.

"I don't want you! Get out of here," said Thomas, his fear starting to rise. "I'll get David after you if you try to get closer. He is my friend, and he will listen to what I have to say."

"Why would he? David is all caught up in the fantasy of God's love—emotional delusion that leaves no room for intellect like yours. Not to mention all that you've achieved and the wonder of your new ideas. Go with him, and any intelligence will be useless. Why do you think he chose that way? I'll tell you why, because his mind operates on a lesser plane than yours. You won't get a decent exchange of ideas in heaven… it's all about love, not about what you have done, or what you can do."

Thomas could see some logic in this line of thought. "What about the sulfur smell? I can't breathe…"

"Oh, that foul place has nothing to do with us. We don't even need to acknowledge its existence. That's where the truly evil people end up. Where I'm from, you can make the air whatever fragrance you like. Come on, and I'll take you to the philosopher's club, a very elite group of thinkers. The aroma from them is what I call the 'great minds' bouquet. I think you'll like it much better than heaven's single boring odor that I call 'O de Serviteur'."

Thomas started to accept the invitation when he thought of the lamb. "Wait, I want to first talk to David about his toy lamb."

"That toy is nothing here… Let me tell you what it is," the voice whispered. "It's an emblem of weakness and shame."

"Not for me," protested Thomas.

"I know," reassured the voice. "It started out a symbol of your cowardice, but you made it into a powerful force for achievement in medicine. For David, it represents an inept attempt at love. He can't even spell the word, let alone know what it means. But I am pleased you broke free from that antiquated sentimentality and used the lamb to your advantage. You proved you are worthy of greatness. Now you're ready to take the next step to rise above this and rule with intellect making great medical discoveries. So let's go. Your colleagues await you."

The mind of Thomas filled with grand thoughts, and he started to follow the voice when from far away Thomas heard a faint song—"Jesus loves me, this I know…"

"Wait, it's David. Before we go, I want to tell him my side of the lamb story. I think it will help him feel good about himself," said Thomas.

The darkness moved in. "Quick, follow me before he can suck you in with lies about God's love. Remember, God failed to intervene when that child died of epiglottitis; so believe me, it's all a hoax. Your mind is too sharp to fall for that Jesus stuff."

David's words reached out, barely audible over the voice of darkness and the thickening mist. "Thomas don't listen to it. Love is what fills me to overflowing. It can do the same for you; that is why I gave you the lamb to share with you the love of God."

The darkness started to recede, wheezing out a final gasp. "You're the one who made good things happen in your life, not some silly child's song and a wooden lamb. I know of a meeting of prominent doctors about to start. Think about what you could learn. Love can't protect you from mistakes, but medical wisdom can." With a final slurp, it faded away.

"It's gone," said David. "But at the first opportunity, it will sneak back. Here in the gray lands you can see and smell the darkness, but back on earth it is far more subtle. Unless you learn to trust the Lord and let His love surround you completely, you will never be free of the darkness or able to breathe in the light. God's love gave me light and allowed me to breathe in my darkness, and I wanted the same for you."

A puzzled look came upon Thomas, "But… I wanted to tell you of all that I accomplished because you gave me that toy lamb—the scientific breakthroughs, my professional success… You don't seem to care about that do you?" Thomas slouched as if the air had leaked from him.

"Jesus cares about you and offers forgiveness for your foolish pride. It's clear you still struggle with loving yourself over God. So by the grace of God, you are being sent back to earth not to do more but to be less."

"Is this going to be another episode in my life?"

"Yes and no, you'll eventually return to your own body, but before that, you have one final moment to witness."

"What words do I say if it gets a little rough and I need to come back to talk with you?"

"Oh, don't go looking for me or you will miss the only one who can truly help you."

"Wait! I am not sure I understand," Thomas called out as he saw David turn and walk toward a warm glow on the horizon.

As he left David began to sing:

"Jesus loves me is my song.
In His flock I do belong.
He is always by my side,
In His care do I abide

I was born a trisomy.
Little hope they gave to me.
In my life He showed His power,
A life of love to Him did flower.

In my hardship He found a way
to fold His love into my clay
Jesus loves me is my glow,

It's all I ever want to know.

After David finished the song he turned, smiled, and spoke to Thomas, "Remember to breathe in faith, hope, and most of all love, and then breathe it out to others."

Whoosh.

Memorial Service

This is David's funeral, but why would David send me here? thought Thomas.

The service progressed, but Thomas couldn't get over having just talked with David and he wondered what a stir it would make if he got up and told them of meeting David in the gray lands. *I don't know that I could convey how he reflects heaven's radiance, or his kingly stature. No, it is better to stay quiet than have people think of me as a deranged man trying to co-opt the service.*

"Now I would like to invite any of you who would like to say something about David to come forward."

After several people had talked about David's amazing ability to lift their spirits, an older man with a walking-cane ambled up and plunked something on the music stand. Turning to face the people he said, "I have known David his entire life. In fact, I was the doctor who delivered him forty-five years ago."

Thomas' jaw dropped. He hadn't recognized Dr. Bennet at first because... he looked old and frail, barely able to walk. All those night-time deliveries had taken a toll, though once he started to speak, Thomas recognized his mentor, for his voice still commanded attention.

"I am ashamed to say that when I delivered David who had obvious Down Syndrome, I thought his life wouldn't amount to much. I counseled Jack and Betty Hansen to let him die instead of putting him through heart surgery. Thank God they ignored my advice. As you can see by looking around, his life meant a great deal to many people beyond his parents. But now let me share with you what David has meant to me.

"Right before I retired, David came to me in my office, not for medical reasons, but as Betty said when she made the appointment, he wanted to meet and thank me for helping him be born. Originally, I thought this would be just another one of the thousands of babies I had delivered over my career, a nice little retirement gesture. When I saw David and Betty walk through the door, the memory of David's birth came blazing back. My harsh pronouncement about David that night pounded me with shame, and I wondered if they wanted to throw those words back at me. Instead, David gave me this." Dr. Bennet held up a little toy lamb. "Then he gave me the biggest hug I have ever had and said, 'Jesu ov me, I'm is eep. Ahhhhhh Yooooo haaaa eep?'"

A knowing laugh sprinkled through the crowd along with tears of remembrance of David saying to them the very same unintelligible words. "Betty helped me understand what David had said, 'Jesus loves me and I'm his sheep; are you His sheep too?' I must tell you, I stood there completely flummoxed by his question. Here I am being hugged by a man I had considered hardly worth anything and being asked by him the most important question of life itself. Not knowing what else to say, I said, 'Yes.' Well, my shame only grew. Here I stood, a doctor of high integrity and had just lied to this simple disabled man. Shame flooded my soul. I could tell David saw through my deception, for he began to cry. Then David took the lamb from my hand, he placed it on my chest and told me, I'm interpreting his words here, 'Jesus loves you and forgives you... I love you too and forgive you too. My life is good and wonderful because of His love. I want to share His love with you."

Dr. Bennet choked up at this point in the story, blew his nose and tried to regain his composure. After a few moments of awkward silence, Jack and Betty went up and gave Dr. Bennet a hug. The whole auditorium became quiet, sensing the power of God's love.

Jack then turned and spoke, "I carved the first lamb for David's twelfth birthday because he had a hard time with words. I wanted him to have it as a visual symbol that Jesus loved him and that his mom and I loved him too. Soon after, he gave it away to one of the kids at school, so I carved another, then another. Over the years, I have carved over five hundred of these lambs because David wanted everyone to know—Jesus loves you,... David loves you,... and that Jesus makes life good with His love." The whole crowd erupted into applause and praise.

Dr. Bennet by then had regained control enough to finish. "I once lost a baby during an emergency C-section. Though I prayed frantically for God to let the child live, the baby died soon after delivery. I couldn't see how a God of love would let that happen, so I turned my back on God's love and labeled Him a fable for weak minds. For most of my life I had believed a good life consisted of achievement and length of years. I now admit my pride utterly blinded me to the truth of God's love." Dr. Bennet lifted the lamb up so all could see it. "We are not here to honor David for his accomplishments, which were few. Instead, we are here because David loved Jesus and wanted to share that love with each person he met. David showed me that life is not about making a name for yourself; it is about loving God first, then loving everyone else. David showed me Jesus that day—God's love that can take a person I had labeled worthless and make him a blessing. A miraculous love that can bring goodness and purpose into any situation. In David's hug, God showed me the power of His love, and I knew I wanted what David had. Through David, God revealed to me the breadth of love and that life without it is nothing more than a passing noise. Soon after Betty and David left my office, I asked Jesus to make me His lamb and fill me with His love like I saw in David. I am here to tell you what David would want all of you to know—life is so very good with the love of God. No length of days can make up for life without God's love, nor will the smallest, most insignificant life negate the greatness of His love. One final thought. When David was born I believed his life was a big mistake, but I now know that with God there are no mistakes. Jesus has used David's life to bless the multitude."

Looking about, Thomas saw people weeping, and many with hands raised clutching a little carved lamb. Thomas gasped, "Oh, for the love of God."

Whoosh…

Beginning with Nothing

Whoosh… beep click whoosh… beep click whoosh. The sound of mechanical breathing penetrated the fog that held Thomas. Beep click whoosh… beep click whoosh… beep click whoosh.

Have I been dreaming? Where am I? Come on, wake up! He struggled, but his body seemed caught in a web of semi-consciousness, not responding to his commands.

"Uhhhhh," Thomas tried to call out for David, but the words stuck, forcing him to gag. *Something is caught in my throat. Get it out. Let me go. What's happening to me?* Panic seized Thomas as he thrashed to free himself. In a short while fatigue set in, and he sank into exhaustion. *Could this be the black hole? O, for the love of God, let me out of here… sweet Jesus help me… Lord have mercy.*

Beep click whoosh… beep click whoosh… beep click whoosh.

Thomas searched for the glow of David, Elena, and Joshua, but something covered his eyes and held them closed. Moving his head, he tried to break free.

"Dr. Jones, good to see you waking up," said a voice off to the side. "I am going to turn off the ventilator. If you breathe on your own, I will remove the endo-tracheal tube. Try not to thrash around, and I will undo your restraints after I pull the tube out."

Beep click whoosh... beep click whoosh... beep click... silence.

Thomas took a breath and struggled to move, but a heaviness dragged on his entire body.

"Good job. One last suction and out comes the tube..."

Sluuurrrrip, the tickle made Thomas gag then cough.

"... Cuff down and tube is out. Now to get you cleaned up. We taped your eyes closed to keep them from drying... once I wipe off the gel, you'll be able to open them... there, that's better. Welcome back to the land of the living."

Opening his eyes, Thomas looked about, then tried to sit up, but promptly flopped down. *Where am I?* flashed in his brain. Surprisingly, he could not figure out how to translate the thought into speech.

The effort to move cleared some of the fog. Thomas began to piece together the where and why of his surroundings. A monitor overhead with a dot of light tracing out a heartbeat. An IV bag hung next to it. Lifting his hand, he saw the restraint around his wrist attached to the hospital bed rail. *Am I back in Sighetu? No, it can't be… there are lights and… I'm in an ICU.* The far end of the room opened onto the nurse's station. A respiratory tech pushed the ventilator out of the room and pulled a white curtain across the opening. A nurse dressed in blue scrubs entered and bent over with a stethoscope to listen to his lungs.

"Now, breathe deep for me. That's it, keep breathing Dr. Jones. You've had quite an ordeal over the last five days," she said, checking the oxygen saturation monitor. "We thought we'd lost you a couple of times, but by some miracle you're alive and here with us at the University CCU. I am your nurse, please call me Chris. I have to check you over, so we'll start with your feet and work up. Let me see you move them. Now your arms."

He saw his right arm rise, but something was missing, though he did not know what.

"Here, let me tap on your left hand… try to move it for me," said Chris.

Thomas felt a tap, tap, somewhere, but couldn't attach the sensation as to coming from

his left hand. *I must still be a ghost in the gray
lands… where is David? Why did the nurse say I
am in the CCU What's happened to me?*

"We'll be moving you out on the medical
floor tomorrow, and you can begin rehab."

"Noooo… yes," Thomas heard his voice
rasp. But despite tremendous effort, only
"Noooo" or "yes" would come out. *My throat; I
can't speak,* reverberated through his mind.

"Dr. Jones, try to relax. If you want, I can
give you something to help you calm down,"
Chris said, putting her hand on Thomas' hand
and giving it a gentle squeeze.

"Yes… No… No." Thomas grew frustrated
at not being able to talk beyond yes and no. He
knew what he wished to say, but couldn't get his
mouth to say it. *I demand to know what has happened to me, not drugs.* He screamed inside, but
only "no" came out.

"You had a heart attack getting off the
plane." Chris said adjusting the IV. "Fortunately,
it didn't happen in the air or you would not be
here. Unfortunately, during the lengthy resuscita-
tion, you probably suffered a stroke causing left

sided weakness. It amazes everyone you're still alive and breathing."

He tried again to move, flinging himself in an attempt to sit up, but his left side didn't respond.

"Whoa there, Dr. Jones, calm down," Chris spoke, putting her hand gently on his shoulder. "You're going to be okay. You just need to give it some time."

Thomas sunk back into his pillow, trying to figure out all that had taken place. *Joshua, Elena, David, was it all a dream from a brain deprived of oxygen? What do I do now? I can't walk or talk—my life is worthless.* A wave of melancholy washed over him. *Why did life do this to me? I have a lot going on, research still to accomplish. I'm not done living! How could this be happening? I have a lot to give humanity, but now… I'm useless.* Thomas glanced at his tray table. Someone had placed his three legged lamb on it. The irony of his medical condition taunted him. *My life had everything going for it and now has nothing. Whereas David had nothing in his life and now has it all. It's not fair!* The lamb stared at him. *What is going on with me? Is this real or…?* He remembered Dr. Bennet holding up the lamb David had given him and saying something about life being so very good because of the love of God. *That's who I should to talk to, my mentor. If he actually spoke at David's funeral, then everything else I have experienced must be true.* Thomas looked intently at the lamb. *Yes, there is one way to know—I must talk to Dr. Bennet.*

The following day, Thomas moved out of the CCU to the rehab unit and met with the therapy team. Each member did a thorough exam. At the end of the day they held a group meeting to pool their findings and develop a therapy treatment plan. Thomas attended the session to gain insight into his condition.

The physical therapist started: "Dr Jones, due to your stroke you have left-sided paralysis and neglect. Forgive me for using laymen's terms, but I wish to make sure you understand. Left-sided neglect means you ignore everything on the left as if it doesn't exist. We will develop a program to help you reconnect with your left side, but it's going to take time. How much comes back is hard to tell."

Next came the occupational therapist. "I'll be working on skills for activities of daily living—self-care, hygiene, feeding and dressing. Learning to do these activities with only the right hand can be daunting at first but not impossible."

The speech therapist then began, "We'll start with swallowing and communication skills. You have expressive aphasia, and though you know what you want to say, it will not form into words. Currently, you can say yes and no, but beyond that your speech becomes garbled except for some swear words. You will have to relearn how to temper your frustration over the lack of being understood. Remember, it is frustrating for both you and your family, so work hard on your patience. We will set up a computer and eye tracking device to enhance your communication as soon as we define what assistance you will need."

The next day the therapy started, and it shocked Thomas how exhausting it proved to be. Learning to communicate proved the most frustrating, mainly because he wanted to talk with his mentor, Dr. Bennet, but couldn't communicate that request. He wanted to say, "I want to see Dr. Bennet." But all that came out of his mouth was

"Yes… yes… no." Thomas finally pointed at letters on a board to spell things, but the effort proved exhausting. On the second day, an eye tracking device with a computer provided Thomas with a means to say what he wanted. Slowly he spelled it out. "i waant to see dr. bennet," droned the computer.

"Good," said the speech therapist, "I will see what I can do to make that happen."

Enlisting the help of the social worker, they arranged for Dr. Bennet to come for a visit the following week.

In the intervening time, Thomas tried to sort through his gyrating thoughts and get them into the computer.

I haven't seen Dr. Bennet in over twenty years. He is going to think I'm demented if I tell him of being in the gray mist with David and the black hole. How can I explain this on a computer that takes me forever to spell out words?… I know! If I show him my lamb and he has a lamb, maybe he'll understand. I can tell him I saw him speak at David's funeral, even though I wasn't there. Even if he thinks I'm crazy, at least I'll know it happened, that I really met Joshua, Elena and David. I won't

tell him about being at David's delivery or he'll real-
ly think I've lost my mind from the stroke.
"Nooooo!" *That won't work. O for the love of God,*
I can't do anything for myself anymore, not even
think... Who am I kidding; all that took place in
the gray land is a dream of an oxygen-deprived
brain... I would be better off dead,... not like this.
But if he does have a lamb like mine...

Fighting off despair became a full-time battle for Thomas. He hated his body for not doing
what he told it to do. His mind once sharp, now
irritatingly slow and forgetful. His anger with
himself only grew.

"You should call your daughter," remarked
one nurse. "She has called quite a few times to
find out how you are doing... You know she
spent the first day of your MI at the hospital
praying for you in the CCU waiting room."

Thomas remembered that he had invited
Robin, his daughter, to the building dedication
hoping to reestablish a relationship with her. But
now... *I don't want her seeing me like this.* "No."

"Oh Dr. Jones, she stayed at your bedside
as long as she could, but when you didn't wake

up, she finally had to return to her classes. She is a sweet young lady. I bet you're proud of her."

"Yes," the only word that escaped from Thomas, though inside, he held great sorrow. *I have missed out on being a loving father for Robin, and now I am stuck in a useless body, more of a burden than a father.* Melancholy swept over him.

The nurse noted his sadness and tried to cheer him. "Don't be so sad, Dr. Jones. Remember, they just named the genetics building in your honor and look at all you have done for medical research. I'm sure your family is very proud of you."

"No, no," Thomas cried, while his mind filled with remorse. *My career means very little now. What good is a building when you can't even wipe yourself without help?*

"No?" puzzled the nurse. "Well, I think you've led an exemplary life. I hope you don't worry too much about your current condition. Many people bounce back with time and therapy. It's amazing how much patients can regain through rehab. I know it may seem dark now, but remember there is light at the end of the tunnel."

Dark tunnel… light? I need to know if what happened in the gray lands is real. Thomas shuddered, thinking about the dark hole. *Is it waiting for me?*

"Dr. Jones, please calm yourself," said the nurse, alarmed at his rise in his blood pressure and pulse. "You don't want to end up back in the CCU or cause…"

"No," Thomas tried to relax. *If only Dr. Bennet really went to David's funeral and spoke, then there is hope for me. Oh, for the love of God, let it be true.*

Two days later, the nurse looked in on Thomas and announced, "Dr. Jones, Dr. Bennet is here to see you." She opened the door and wheeled Dr. Bennet in, stopping the wheelchair at the bedside. He looked old and feeble but smiled at Thomas and stuck out his hand. Noting Thomas' difficulty, he clasped his forearm.

"Thomas, it is good to see you. We haven't talked since you left for the NIH in Washington over twenty years ago. I heard they named the research building after you. How was the dedication?… I mean… I am sorry about your MI and stroke. I hope you recover soon… Forgive my bedside manner, it has gotten old like everything else. As you can see, I'm stuck in this contraption, can't even walk on my own anymore."

Thomas brushed aside the small-talk, not wanting to waste time being polite. He had to ask the question that weighed heavily upon him, "Yes, aaaammm!"

"What? Say it again, my hearing is not great even with these hearing aids."

"Yes, laaammmb!" Thomas frantically pulled over the computer the occupational therapist had set up. Hitting the spacebar with his right index finger lit up the screen with the question he had worked on since being told of Dr. Bennet's visit. "Yes, yes!" His fears mixed with excitement. Finally, he pressed the key to make the computer read aloud his question.

A robotic voice said, "Did David Hansen give you a toy lamb and tell you—'Jesus loves me, I'm his sheep; are you His sheep too?'"

Dr. Bennet sat there, astonishment crossed his face. Then he spoke, "How did you know about that? We haven't spoken to each other in years." Dr Bennet twisted in the wheelchair and pulled out a lamb from his pocket. "I brought it because I wanted to tell you the story of this lamb. How I got it from one of my former patients, David Hansen, and what it means to me."

"YES!" Thomas looked around for his lamb, then remembered the nurse had stuck it in his left hand. Using his right hand, he pulled out his left from under the sheet. Clenched in his hand, the lamb poked out. Carefully, Thomas pried his fingers loose to show his own lamb with three legs.

"Well, I'll be danged," said Dr. Bennet. "Did you get this from David? How did you ever meet him? You haven't lived in this area for forty years."

"Yes, yes!" exclaimed Thomas. "Yes, yes, Jesu o yes," Tears began streaming down his face. "Yes eep, Ahhhhhh Yooooo haaaa eep?"

"What did you just say?" asked Dr Bennet. "You sound just like David when he gave me this sheep."

It shocked Thomas to hear his voice struggling from the stroke. He thought of David, Elena, and Joshua, and their struggles in life. *Yet with all their hardships, God found a way.* Suddenly, out of nowhere, a verse came to Thomas: "Blessed are the poor in spirit, for theirs is the kingdom of heaven."

That's the verse the stranger gave to Joshua! Yes, it is for me too. Thomas prayed, crying and laughing at the same time. *I have seen it with my own eyes in Joshua, Elena, and David—theirs is the kingdom of heaven. How good is that?*

Not fully aware of all that Thomas had experienced, Dr. Bennet spoke, "I find it a little difficult to admit this, but I must tell you. For most of my life, I pursued being a good doctor, but in my great effort at life I missed the point of life. You see, I had never received God's love. I did not understand its power to make what we consider worthless into the glorious. That is, until David showed me with this lamb and gave me a hug filled with forgiveness. I delivered David and considered his life useless, not worth the air he breathed. Because of his Down Syndrome, I thought he would only live in an institution for whatever few years he had. Truth is, God's love makes all the difference. For the love of God can take someone like myself, a stubborn know-it-all, take all the wind from their sails and then breathe in newness of life." At this point Dr. Bennet stopped to choke back tears, "Through David and his loving hug, God changed a foolish old man who had cursed Jesus, into one of His own. That's what I call amazing grace."

"Yes," exclaimed Thomas, bursting with excitement. "Yes, yes!"

Dr. Bennet continued, "I can't explain it, but I know it is true. Jesus forgave me and let me be His sheep… I know all this sounds childish, but I have to tell you… Jesus loves me, this I know."

"Yes, Jesus loves me, yes, Jesus loves me…" the song tumbled from Thomas' mouth without impediment, much to the surprise of Thomas and Dr. Bennet. *I can sing!* "Yes, Jesus loves me. Yes, Jesus loves me," Thomas sang over and over.

"Thomas let me speak for a moment. I'm asking you to forgive me for being a poor example of a doctor. I fear I taught you to discount the spiritual side of life calling it foolishness, when, in fact, the love of Jesus makes life,… well, Life."

"Yes, yes," responded Thomas.

"Jesus loves me is my song
In His flock I now belong
He is always by my side

In His care do I abide."

"Hey, you two are having quite a party in here," said the nurse, sticking her head into the room. "Sorry to break it up, but Dr. Bennet's ride is here."

After Dr. Bennet left, the nurse returned to check on Thomas. "Did you and Dr. Bennet have a nice chat?"

"Yes!"

"You seemed pretty apprehensive this morning. Are you doing better now?"

"Yes, yes, yes."

"Anything else you need right now?"

"Yes,... I... ah..."

"Here, use your computer to type it out. I'll be back in a few minutes." The nursed pushed the computer over to Thomas and left.

Thomas with great effort, using the eye tracking, typed out: "I want to see my daughter."

When the nurse returned, she read the note.

"That's great, I'll ask her next time she calls. In the meantime, work on what you want to say and type it out on the computer. The more you use it, the better you will get."

When she left, Thomas stared at the computer screen. "iiiiiiiiiiii," shot across the top. He closed his eyes to stop generating nonsense and think of what to say. How to explain all that had happened and all that had changed.

God, I am not sure what to say. I have spent my life condemning You for not acting with love, though it is I who failed to act in love. I see now that love is courageous, and I have been a coward. Starting with David when he was being bullied by Carl, and sadly, also with my family. I realize now that I've been acting from fear of rejection rather than love—always trying to gain others' respect and prove my worth.

I mistook that toy lamb as a symbol of what I needed to do. I thought I could show You, the creator of all things, how to make a better world. Instead, I hurt my family, and probably many others along the way. I desire to change, but I don't know how to start. So, along with Joshua, I ask for your mercy and forgiveness, and like Elena, I want to place my hope in Your unfailing love.

Ironically, it has taken the loss of my health and nearly dying for me to find out what life is about. My heart attack and the stroke have taken away everything I held dear, and through this ordeal You have shown me Your love. It is strange and humbling to say this—Thank You for Your merciful blessing of my illness.

It is amazing that, through all David's disabilities, You showed Your love to hundreds of people, and thus, his poor life became rich in Your glory. In contrast, I pushed myself to achieve greatness, thinking it would somehow make up for my cowardice and my many mistakes. In so doing, I reflected vain glory instead of true glory and thus helped no one. My accolades did nothing except to spread blindness to myself and to those who applauded me. Now, with a weak heart and a damaged brain, I am grateful for what has happened, if by it I can come to partake in Your everlasting love that I saw in David, a man after Your own heart.

Thomas opened his eyes and took a deep breath. "Yes…" then began to sing:

"Jesus loves me, this I know.

By His grace I'm free to go,

Walk in the light and never leave,

For of His love I've learned to breathe."

Thank You Jesus, he prayed, *please, help me share the right words with my daughter that we might breathe the air of heaven together for all eter-nity.*

Chapter 7 - Epilogue

With my daughter's encouragement and with her loving help, I have written of my encounters with Joshua, Elena, and David that others may benefit as I have. It is the least I could do for the great mercy I have been shown. For those who knew these amazing people on earth, I pray that you join me and rejoice with heaven for their wonderful lives.

I admit that a life living with a stroke is not easy. I get frustrated which leads to depression and my mind being bombarded with lies and accusations from the pit. One of my accuser's favorite is:

You were a doctor with a great mind; now look at you. Not worth the air you breathe. Why you'd be better off dead than depending on someone to take care of you, to wipe the drool from your mouth. You're a burden and a drag on life. Everyone is just waiting for you to die.

I must say the evil tirade makes breathing difficult. At those times I pray with the writer of Psalm 88.

"O Lord, the God who saves me,

day and night I cry out before you.
May my prayer come before you; turn your
ear to my cry.
For my soul is full of trouble
and my life draws near the grave.
I am counted among those who go down
to the pit;
I am like a man without strength."

I find it reassuring that the anguish I feel
from my stroke and heart attack is captured within
this prayer written three thousand years ago. It
gives words for my feelings, and by these lines I
know God understands my depression and frustrations
on being stuck in this damaged body. I
have repeatedly asked Him to heal me and trust
that He will someday, but for now I am learning
to trust in Him, one breath at a time.

There are periods in this hard journey
when I panic and don't want to go on. That is
when lies from within urge me to take an easy
way out in death. In those dark moments of fear I
review the lessons Joshua, Elena, and David
taught me on breathing heaven's air. I can hear

Elena singing "Jesus loves me," followed by her beautiful song of hope:

> "Death ruled and had me chained,
> shrouded in the awful dark,
> But hope in His unfailing love,
> lit a humble spark.
> At first a smoldering wick—
> hope burning 'gainst the night.
> Jesus' mighty love the fuel,
> made my hope grow ever bright.
> With faith in His unfailing love,
> Oh, what a wondrous sight.
> shining forth till it leads me home,
> Hope the light of life."

In times of despair I call out "Lord have mercy," and take a deep breath letting the air of God's mercy fill my soul. *Darkness get away from me for I am His child, pure and holy.* Then, I exhale slowly, followed by breathing in "O sweet Jesus," the hope I have in the risen Lord. As I hold it in, the beauty of Jesus begins to replace my ugliness. I am His, and He is mine. As my second breath seeps out, I anticipate the third most wonderful breath of all— "O for the love of God." His love reaches deeper than my deepest pit and redeems me to be His sheep forever. I trust His love for me will overcome all my deficiencies. Psalm 33 has become my psalm:

> "But the eyes of the Lord are on those who
> fear Him,
> on those whose hope is in his unfailing
> love,
> to deliver them from death
> and keep them alive in famine.
> We wait in hope for the Lord;
> he is our help and our shield.
> In him our hearts rejoice,
> for we trust in his holy name.
> May your unfailing love rest upon us, O
> Lord,
> even as we put our hope in you."
> Psalm 33:18-22

I'm confident that Joshua, Elena, and David are cheering me on in my learning to breathe. Even better is the knowledge that God is cheering for me because He loves me and is with me in all my ways even the dark valleys of a stroke.

"Jesus loves me, this I know for the Bible tells me so—"

"He who did not spare his own Son, but gave him up for us all—how will he not also, along with him, graciously give us all things?" Romans 8:32 NIV

"Therefore we do not lose heart. Though outwardly we are wasting away, yet inwardly we are being renewed day by day. For our light and momentary troubles are achieving for us an eternal glory that far outweighs them all. So we fix our eyes not on what is seen, but on what is unseen. For what is seen is temporary, but what is unseen is eternal." 2 Corinthians 4:16-18 NIV

A special thanks to David's family for talking with me and giving permission to tell of his life. My hope is that you will not pass up having faith in the Lord's mercy, knowing the hope we

352

have in Jesus. But most of all, may you come to understand the tremendous love God has for you in Jesus the Christ.

Jesu lov me, I'm is eep. Ahhhhhh Yooooo haaaa eep too?

"Three things will last forever—faith, hope, and love—and the greatest of these is love."
1 Corinthians 13:13 NLT

www.ingramcontent.com/pod-product-compliance
Lightning Source LLC
Chambersburg PA
CBHW072119250626
47159CB00007B/2496